Galileo's
Theme Park

Third Flatiron Anthologies
Volume 7, Book 23, Summer 2018

Edited by Juliana Rew
Cover Art by Keely Rew

Galileo's Theme Park

Third Flatiron Anthologies
Volume 7, Summer 2018

Published by Third Flatiron Publishing
Juliana Rew, Editor and Publisher

Copyright 2018 Third Flatiron Publishing
ISBN #978-1-7322189-4-9

Discover other titles by Third Flatiron:

(1) Over the Brink: Tales of Environmental Disaster
(2) A High Shrill Thump: War Stories
(3) Origins: Colliding Causalities
(4) Universe Horribilis
(5) Playing with Fire
(6) Lost Worlds, Retraced
(7) Redshifted: Martian Stories
(8) Astronomical Odds
(9) Master Minds
(10) Abbreviated Epics
(11) The Time It Happened
(12) Only Disconnect
(13) Ain't Superstitious
(14) Third Flatiron's Best of 2015
(15) It's Come to Our Attention
(16) Hyperpowers
(17) Keystone Chronicles
(18) Principia Ponderosa
(19) Cat's Breakfast
(20) Strange Beasties
(21) Third Flatiron Best of 2017
(22) Monstrosities

License Notes

www.thirdflatiron.com

Contents

*****~~~~~*****

Editor's Note

by Juliana Rew

It is with great pleasure that we embark on our twenty-third themed anthology. Third Flatiron presents *Galileo's Theme Park,* a new collection of science fiction, space opera, dark fantasy, horror, and humor, in which twenty international authors write about how the universe has changed since Humanity took a closer look at the stars. We asked contributors to take us on a speculative journey to the lands beyond Earth revealed to us by Galileo and other space scientists.

Have you ever seen the moon? Recently columnist Leonard Pitts Jr. praised a video he'd seen describing how writer and amateur astonomer Wylie Overstreet had set up his telescope on the streets of Los Angeles and was amazed at the reactions from passersby as the looked at the moon. The exclamations of the many strangers who stopped to peek through his telescope reminded us of our common awe when witnessing cosmic events up close, such as last summer's total eclipse. "A New View of the Moon" was directed by Alex Gorosh and is part of *The Atlantic Selects,* an online showcase of short documentaries from independent creators, curated by *The Atlantic.* The video is currently available for viewing at https://www.youtube.com/watch?v=ZV89qH9IGrA

Many of us wonder whether we are alone in the universe. The lonely astronaut in Alex Zalben's "And Yet They Move" is about to find out. And Erica Ruppert's protagonist in "Signals" keeps hearing music—is it of the spheres?

The power of prayer makes a lasting impression in more than one story here. In Neil James Hudson's "New Heaven, New Earth," an interstellar expedition seeks to find whether the god of an encroaching Ptolemeic universe will accept Humanity's petition.

What if these prayers were answered? In G. D. Watry's "First, They Came As Gods," a priest and a scientist debate whether the discovery of extraterrestrial life on Jupiter's volcanic moon Io will change our view of our place in the universe. A disembodied being from another of Jupiter's moons shows itself to Galileo's assistant in Dr. Jackie Ferris's "Vincenzo, the Starry Messenger."

But even if there is other intelligent life, is it so far away that we may never actually meet? Waiting becomes a theme in more than one story. Humanity's hope and patience finally pay off in Jo Miles's inspiring "And the Universe Waited."

Though Galileo's pronouncements got him in hot water with the Catholic Church of the 16th century, little did he know that his far-seeing telescope would become a thing of the past, as in Adrik Kemp's planet-towing grunts in "Titanrise." In a future where money buys everything, Ginger Strivelli's rich industrialists guide space exploration in ways that suit them best in "For the Love of Money." And Jemima Pett's tour guide tells the adventurous among us why "Titan is All the Rage."

For a touch of horror, Steve Toase offers an alternate history explaining how the Russians get to space first, in "The Kromlau Gambit." A recurrent theme in some "slipstream" science fiction is the ominous planet that seems inimical to human life, for example, in Elena Arsenieva's "A Birch Tree, A White Fox," or the new "A Quiet Place" movie, where anyone who speaks immediately dies. Justin Short's disturbing "Dispatches from the Eye of the Clowns" continues down that strange road.

Little green men from Mars do a creditable job of imitating "Tam O 'Shanter" (aka Scotland's version of "Sleepy Hollow") in Connie Vigil Platt's "Night on the

High Desert," set in the Old West. In "The Beast and the Orb of Earth Deux," Wendy Nikel's podcasters expose a mysterious orb found in space.

Space opera is terrific when it involves a no-holds-barred space battle amid black holes, and that's what Eric J. Guignard gives us in spades, in "A Hard-Fought Episode at the TON-1 Black Hole."

Ultimately, we realize we are only small players in the cosmic circus. We close our short story section with two touching tales of the end of the world as we know it: "Growing Smaller" by Jimmy Huff and "The Bright and Hollow Sky" by Martin M. Clark.

SCORE! We have some of the funniest writers around in our Grins & Gurgles (Flash Humor) section. Granted, a couple of their tales involve arms being ripped out of sockets, like Ville Nummenpää's "No Encore" and Art Lasky's "Just Right Guy," but physical humor is the best, right? If slapstick's not your bag, there's plenty of amusement to be found in hobbies such as cooking and birdwatching. Look for Rachel Rodman's "Devouring the Classics: Ten Recipes" and Lisa Timpf's "Advice for the 2060s Birder."

Seven writers are making another appearance in a Third Flatiron Anthology, showing their versatility and popularity with our Readers. We are also excited that nearly half of our authors this time are women.

We hope you'll enjoy this excellent selection, inspired by the worlds opened to us by the great Galileo Galilei.

Juliana Rew
June 2018

*****~~~~~*****

9

And Yet They Move

by Alex Zalben

Angela lay on the beach on a planet in the middle of an impossible solar system and waited for the tide to wash over her until she floated away.

She listened to the crash of the waves as they slammed into the shore, methodically washing away grains of tiny red sand. Angela pictured herself as one of those grains, a tiny speck in the center of her own universe. Only there was no one else on the beach with her, no one on the planet or in the solar system. Only Angela, all alone, light years away from the nearest human being.

She stuck her fingers in the red sand next to her and felt the granules rush and fall as she wiggled her digits in the coolness, creating mountains that crumbled into valleys in the blink of an eye.

That was all Pisa-5 was, sand and waves; vast, empty oceans and more specks of dark, red sand the color of blood than there were stars in the sky.

Angela sighed at the metaphor, because of course that wasn't accurate, of course there were more stars. She pictured her father's withering glance at the thought, felt the sting of his disdain at her artistic flights of fancy.

Galileo's Theme Park

"There's no room for art in science," he would scold her, gesturing to change her display from ancient music videos or old paintings (Angela loved everything from Renaissance, to Dada) to more acceptable equations and courses of study.

Angela's imagination, her love of music, always felt to her like the things that held her back from greatness. She had always daydreamed through lessons as a child and could coast on her natural intelligence. While a teacher would drone on about something she had studied and memorized days earlier, she would replay old songs by Michael Jackson (her favorite) in her head. But joining the Global Space Service had widened her world and taught her a more important yet devastating lesson: she was not the smartest person in the room.

It had been her dream to see the stars, to innovate and discover like the scientists of old. It seemed so romantic, the perfect marriage of what she was good at (math) and what she loved (art, and even more than art, music). But in no uncertain terms she had been told those times were long gone, should not be spoken of, ever.

Instead, the GSS put its faith in computers and devices. "The almighty screen," Angela would sometimes whisper bitterly to herself, through the umpteenth demonstration of a program that would "revolutionize" humanity's incessant need to propagate throughout their otherwise empty solar system. They weren't scientists, in Angela's opinion, they were viruses, shuttling slick metal pods around the universe and maintaining the works, reading the readouts and trusting what the computers spat out over their own eyes.

In this, she was alone, and felt the ache of that loneliness. She had no friends at the GSS, only colleagues who seemed happy to check in and out every day, trading their work screens for their home screens.

So when an opportunity arose to travel to Pisa-5, Angela immediately volunteered.

12

And Yet They Move

"Are you sure?" her supervisor had asked. He was a believer in the truth of computers like the rest of them, but she appreciated his occasional empathy. "This is, essentially, a one-way trip. By the time you get back, everyone you know and love will be dead."

Angela stifled a laugh when she heard that—it wouldn't have been appropriate—because she had no one. Her parents had died years earlier, her father given what amounted to a parade by the GSS elite (she often suspected it was her father's name more than her own natural ability that kept her employed). She had nothing except a box-sized apartment filled with a mattress, a desk, and the old, unplayable records she had managed to collect over time. Though it was impossible to find a record player, and even digital music had long ago gone out of vogue, she liked to look at the covers. Sometimes she stared at the cover of Jackson's "HIStory" for hours, analyzing whether the statue on the front was looking towards the future, or back to the past.

Otherwise, everything else in her life Angela had delivered and disposed of through her apps. Like everyone else.

So she had left Earth, the sole human occupant of a probe named the Santa Croce, rocketed at near lightspeed towards an alien planet that seemed to defy every law of physics. Her mission was simple: remain in hypersleep until the ship arrived; fix anything that had broken or would impede the probe's recordings; and otherwise let the Santa Croce do what it was built to do. After exactly a year of studying the planet, she would return to hypersleep and the probe would return to Earth.

Only, Angela wasn't going to be on board.

Instead, a day before the Santa Croce was scheduled to return, she had taken a pod down to the surface of Pisa-5 and decided that she would die the way she lived: utterly alone.

What did she have back on Earth, anyway? A planet ruled by computers, filled with humans who worshipped their interfaces. Prayed to their screens, lived by them. It would be worse now, she decided, decades from when she left. Instead, she lay in the sand and let the waves wash over her. Drowning wouldn't be pleasant, but at least it would be unique: nobody had ever died on this planet before, because no life had existed here before.

Angela could feel the crushed stone of the beach tickling the hair on the back of her neck. Looking up, she could see the moons of Pisa-5 as they arced across the sky. That was normal enough, but what made Pisa-5 unique, what made it *impossible,* was that every other planet in the solar system, and even the sun, revolved around the planet.

When the GSS first detected the system around Pisa-5, there was panic, mostly surrounding the idea that something was wrong with their sensors. Then a greater panic, as the computers couldn't explain why or how Pisa-5 acted the way it did: it challenged the heliocentric model that had dominated science for centuries. It was decided that up-close probing would be necessary to prove this was just an error, and five years later they were ready to launch.

The only personal belonging Angela had taken with her to the planet was a telescope. It was old and worn, made of wood with brass connections and knobs, and when she had begged her father to buy her one as a child (she had seen a painting by a man named H.J. Detouche of one from 1754 that had seared into her memory) he had laughed: what did she need a tiny telescope for, when their sensors were so much more powerful?

But he had relented and tracked down an antiquities dealer to get her one for her sixteenth birthday—her father wasn't all coldness, sometimes his love did shine through, though instances were few and far between—and she had kept that telescope by her side ever since.

Angela reached her hand, the one that wasn't buried in sand, over to feel the telescope on her other side. She traced the metal, feeling where it had chipped and broken, and carefully swiped her fingertip on the glass.

Better clean that, she thought, and laughed because it barely mattered. She could feel the chill of the surf as it washed over her feet now. It was almost time.

Angela shivered, and her mind wandered to the problem of the impossible system. The issue wasn't necessarily that the system rotated around Pisa-5; a large enough planet with a strong enough gravitational pull could, in theory, do that. But Pisa-5 was about the size of Mars, and the fact that Angela could comfortably walk on the surface without flattening into a pancake was proof the gravity wasn't working overtime, either.

The sun was an issue. Centuries earlier scientists had realized a heliocentric model wasn't just *a* possibility, it was the *only* possibility. Time, and additional discovery, had proven them correct. The amount of mass needed to keep a star stable was so great that if a planet dwarfed it in size, it would then be sucked directly into the star.

Potentially, multiple orbs could have the ability to exert a gravitational pull on each other, so three bodies (a star and two planets, say) could work together in a type of circular pull. But that was massively unstable—even a small meteor passing through could knock one of the orbs off its rotational axis—and even with years of theories, the GSS had discovered no evidence this scenario had ever occurred.

Yet somehow, Pisa-5 was the center of this system. Everything rotated around this dead, otherwise completely normal, planet.

The sensors on the Santa Croce had detected nothing out of the ordinary. Angela checked every day for anomalies, because she was supposed to, that's what she was trained to do. But every day for a year the results had come back the same. Every day she would head down the slick metal hall to visit the glass display at the front of the probe. She would look "through" the display, Pisa-5 filling the entirety of the screen in the front (it looked like a window, but like every wall of the ship was only a way of accessing the central computer) and read the results: system normal. Every time.

Three-hundred sixty-four days of this, and she had come to loathe the ship, the screen, the planet, and most of all herself. When the probe returned, she would go back to being nothing and no one. She hadn't proved anything or discovered anything. The computers would be judged accurate, the solar system disregarded as an anomaly, and she would go back to her one room apartment and order-in dinners and existence without meaning. When she pictured home, she pictured her records, and specifically the face of Jackson on the cover of his "Bad" album, staring at her, judging her. It made her feel sick.

Better to do something with her life, even if it was to be the first human to die on Pisa-5. The water was up to her hips now, and she bit her lip to hold back a tear. She wasn't going to cry, not for her life, not for anything.

She grabbed the telescope and lifted it to her right eye. Squinting the other one, she looked up at the stars and marveled at their beauty. Even if the GSS has reduced everything to by-the-book texts and rules, she still gasped every time she saw the wide expanse of the universe.

So Angela looked at the stars, and waited for it all to end. The waves crashed rhythmically, almost making music as they hit the beach, then again as the riptide pulled the water back with a "woosh." Idly, Angela began to hum along with the waves, a noteless tune that nonetheless seemed familiar.

The telescope briefly went black, as if a leaf had blown past it, and Angela removed it from her eye to check for obstructions. There was nothing there. Placing it carefully again, she looked through, then turned her gaze to one of the moons caught in Pisa-5's orbit.

Angela gasped. What she saw didn't seem possible, but there was so much that didn't seem possible about this place. It looked to her eye, through the telescope, like a long, thin tube was extended from the moon, and past the horizon. Removing the telescope again, it wasn't visible, then when she looked through the lens there it was.

Heart pounding, she pivoted to one of the other moons, and sure enough, a tube, headed straight for the planet's surface.

How had these not been visible from space? Perhaps she had been too close to the planet—that's what the Santa Croce had been tasked to study, not the system; and only now, taking the wider view, was she able to see the truth.

She looked from heavenly body to heavenly body, her breath coming quicker, and it was clear that they were all connected to the planet. She looked, carefully, at the side of the sun, not directly at it (even when getting ready to die, she still didn't want to go blind). Sure enough, another long tube.

In her mind, she pictured what it must look like from the edge of the system, all those tubes connected to one main fulcrum, the planet Pisa-5. It looked like something, something she knew. . . And then just like that she saw it in her mind: a model of a solar system. Not a heliocentric model, but a geocentric one. The model used by the Ancient Greeks and believed by religions and scientists for centuries until the truth of heliocentrism came crashing down.

This wasn't a system at all, Angela realized. It was a giant model. That's how it worked, that's why it seemed to defy physics. It was a toy.

And with that came another revelation, one that made her burst into the tears she had been holding back, the salt water streaming down the sides of her face and mingling with the surf that now was up to her shoulders.

I know that music, Angela thought, and then yelled out loud. "I know this music! I know this song!"

Wet and sobbing, she held tight to her telescope and propped herself with the other hand. She ran back to the pod across the beach, away from the surf. She would take the pod to the ship, and then home. They wouldn't want to hear what she had found, might even try to destroy her for telling them. But she would tell them anyway. They needed to know. Everyone needed to know.

The pod door closed, and the rocket flared up beneath, ready to send Angela back.

On the beach, the waves continued to gently tap out their song, a song that could only be created by a tide perfectly manipulated by the gravitational pull of the bodies rotating in harmony around Pisa-5.

You are not alone, the planet sang, over and over again. *You Are Not Alone.*

About the Author

Alex Zalben is the author of an all-ages comic series for Marvel, "Thor and the Warriors Four." For the past decade he's hosted the live show and podcast *Comic Book Club*, which has been profiled in the *New York Times*. He currently works as Managing Editor at Decider.com, with previous bylines on *TV Guide, MTV News,* and more.

*****~~~~~*****

For the Love of Money

by Ginger Strivelli

Maxwell had paid his way onto the first interstellar space flight from Earth like everyone else. He wasn't an astronaut, scientist, or diplomat. He was a hedge fund manager, and a very successful one. There were no career astronauts, scientists, or diplomats on board the Neighborly as Earth sent her and her unlikely crew across the vast emptiness of space to land on the fifth planet in the newly discovered star system.

There had been some people back on Earth who balked at letting billionaires buy their way onto the Neighborly, but no nation's space program could have afforded the huge price of the mission otherwise. So the real scientists trained the billionaires to fly the mission and sent them out on the state-of-the-art faster-than-light ship to the nearby star system, in search of our nearest neighbors. That is why they dubbed the first manned interstellar spaceship, Neighborly.

Maxwell had gotten the post of Mission Commander the same way he got his ticket on the ship, by buying it. He had paid five billion more than the others who'd all just paid ten billion each. He was the richest of the billionaire crew of four, if not the most qualified, though none of them were at all qualified, so it made no difference. The Mission Specialists were a banker and oil tycoon's heir. The Pilot was a real estate mogul turned reality tv star. It was an unusual crew. It was an unusual mission, though. Humanity had finally answered the age-old question, "Are we alone." We had found out that we are not alone, and we were finally going next door to meet our nearest neighbors.

Maxwell of course would get to be the first to set foot on Spintax, what the natives called their planet. He would be the one to speak with the first Spintaxian. He was so proud to be making history and had spent most of the two-week trip through the wormhole, writing and rewriting his first words to say upon touching down. He wanted to go with something that would outshine the old, "One small step for man. . ." line. Alas, when the time came, he was so awestruck he just said, "Hello."

The Spintaxians had sent their United Nations President of the Year, a lady named Caregg, to meet the humans. She waxed poetic about their ship being named "Neighborly" and how she hoped the two planets would become the best of friends, not just good neighbors. Those first historical words from of both sides, were spoken for the record and out of the way. The Spintaxians took the Neighborly's crew to a welcoming party at their world government headquarters.

Maxwell and the rest of the human crew were introduced to representatives from all eighteen continents on Spintax, who proved to be from nine very varied races. Maxwell, rather rudely, though unintentionally so, commented that a couple of the races were so different they seemed more like animals than people. The Spintaxians took no offence, luckily. However when they told him that they used no money, and he said that was incredibly ignorant, a few did seem miffed.

They tried to explain to the humans that on Spintax, one's wealth was determined by how loved they were. Only those few who were hateful and mean to others, making no one care for them, lived in poverty.

Anyone who was loved and cared for by others had all their needs met, and those much loved by many others were rewarded with the trappings of wealth. Though such people gave so much of that wealth away to others, they still never lived too extravagantly. Then, all that charity only made them more loved, which only brought them more wealth. So, Caregg explained, most Spintaxians lived pretty much like their peers, with no high class and no low class, just a good amount of class for all. Of course, the hedge fund manager, banker, oil tycoon's heir, and real estate mogul all found this system totally unfathomable.

Spintax United Nations President of the Year Caregg tried to steer the conversation to the healing arts and Spintax's great accomplishments in eliminating most diseases and healing almost any injury. She bragged that the average life span had increased from eighty-eight years to over one hundred and twenty just in the last century. Nonetheless, that too went badly as the humans couldn't understand how doctors and scientists looking for disease cures weren't paid millions of dollars for their work, or how everyone could afford the treatments that made such long lifespans possible and productive. So she tried again and told them about Spintax's wonderful International Parks but that just led to a discussion of drilling, logging, and mining not being allowed in the parks, and all the profit that left uncollected by the people the humans still couldn't quite understand not wanting to get rich.

Caregg finally managed to get the humans off the awkward subject of their two planets' vastly different financial systems by having the humans join in with a folk dance group that was representing the icy continent of their south pole. Caregg thankfully wrapped up the uncomfortable dinner party after that dance so the visitors could be checked into their guest houses.

21

Maxwell and the banker were hosted by a trash collector. The humans marveled at his beautiful home, and again struggled to understand how one's wealth was based upon how much they were loved, not how much money they earned for their job. They could not make any sense of a trashman living so grandly. Luckily, the trash collector also loved sports, and the humans found common ground with him there, and they began to bond watching a baseball-like sport contest on a tv-like system for a few minutes, until the banker asked the Spintaxian how much the athletes got paid. The conversation took the same dark turns from there, leading the humans and the Spintaxians into the same dispute, before both sides huffed off to bed annoyed and perplexed by the aliens.

Across town the real estate mogul and the oil tycoon's heir were having a similar argument over their host, an artist, telling them that games of chance and fundraising were unheard of on Spintax. No one needed to risk meager earnings to try to win a big payout, or needed to beg others to fund things they or the community needed, as everyone had what they needed, and no one had to wish for more. The artist had lost her temper with the humans and sent them to bed with a less-than-hospitable "good night."

The next morning, the human crew was set to tour one of Spintax's most famous tourist sites. It was an ancient temple complex of pyramids and obelisks that dated back over 10,000 years. Maxwell admonished Caregg for the site having no entrance fee, but otherwise the tour went wonderfully, until the oil tycoon's heir noticed that the site's temples were covered in gold, real pure gold! That just led to another discussion of money, or the lack of money in the Spintax culture. Poor Caregg tried her best to refocus the humans onto the history and mystery of the site, but they were unable to get past the lack of profiteering from it.

For the Love of Money

The next day, Caregg had high hopes of engaging the humans better by taking them to meet a classroom full of children. Alas, the banker took the chance to lecture the children on compounded interest and profitable investment schemes, when a child asked him about his job back on Earth. To which the children, their teacher, and Caregg all took exception, telling the humans no one needed to borrow or invest or save for their retirement on Spintax, because everyone's needs were met, as long as they were not a nasty person no one cared for.

The next day a haggard Caregg took the humans to her own family farm and showed them the animals and crops. She resisted any baiting to discuss finances at all, and kept redirecting the conversation to agriculture, but the billionaires, of course, had little interest in that.

Each day of the fourteen-day visit progressed much the same. The humans stumbled over the concept that what everyone got, they earned by being loved, rather than earned in currency amounts based upon their job or investments. By halfway through the visit, most Spintaxians who had been in contact with the humans had little love for them, finding them greedy, selfish, and materialistic. The humans similarly thought rather poorly of the Spintaxians they met, finding them entitled, carefree, and unambitious. It was a tense last few days, but at long last the humans boarded the Neighborly to return to Earth. Caregg again waxed poetic about their having learned so much about each other's cultures, and hoping for more exchanges of visitors in the future. Maxwell, similar to his simple "hello" greeting, answered her this time with a simple "goodbye."

Maxwell closed the door of the ship and turned to his crewmates with an exaggerated groan. "Can you believe these crazy people?"

"It is such an unfair system, rewarding the lazy and the friendly instead of the smart and the driven," the real estate mogul said.

"We can't tell Earth about these fools! The idiots back there will want to adopt this stupid system of rewarding love instead of working and investing to make money," the oil tycoon's heir said, rolling his eyes.

"Moreover, we have to be sure they don't stay in contact with Earth. Our Earth can never learn of their warped ideals of love," the banker added, saying the last word as if it stung his mouth.

"What are we going to do?" Maxwell said. "They plan to send a ship to Earth with a crew like us to explore our culture. That can't happen. We can't risk them infecting Earth with their madness. We can't risk our whole financial system collapsing into this sort of nonsense."

"We just have to destroy Spintax," the oil tycoon's heir said calmly.

"Exactly!" the real estate mogul spat. "We gotta put these animals down."

The four humans all shook their heads, as if they doubted their agreement, but they all did agree. They planned to destroy a whole planet, a whole culture, multiple races of people, all to protect their money and the culture of money back on Earth. They were all ready to do that. They were all willing to do that. They all just didn't know if they were able to do that. Not being scientists, they didn't even know where to start to try to undo a whole planet.

As they launched into orbit, preparing to head home across cold dark space, they discussed stripping off Spintax's ozone layer, but didn't know how. They discussed triggering a nuclear war, but didn't know how. They discussed creating a black hole to suck the planet into oblivion, but of course they didn't know how to do that either. They even discussed poisoning the Spintaxians with some disease, but they hadn't thought to bring any smallpox-laden blankets to give to the natives.

Finally, as the computer reported they were in Spintax orbit, the real estate mogul, their pilot, spoke up. "What about this wormhole drive thing?" The nerds at NASA taught me to be sure we were well outside of the solar system before I fired it up to create the wormhole. What if I fire it up right here, in orbit above Spintax?"

"Will that destroy the planet?" Maxwell asked. "Do you think that could work?"

"I dunno." Their pilot shrugged. "I just know I'm not supposed to do it."

"Let's try it, then." Maxwell said tightening the seatbelts of his seat.

Just like that, the four humans decided to try to destroy the first planet of neighbors humanity had found. It was just that simple for them, just that matter-of-fact. None of the four had the slightest hesitation. None of them grappled with the moral questions that begged to be asked. They were all in with the real estate mogul's gamble for how to commit genocide. None of them even stopped to think that such a trick might destroy the ship and themselves instead of, or as well as, the planet.

They weren't scientists. They didn't expect the wormhole to throw them back in time, instead of destroying the planet. So, they were rather shocked, when the Neighborly lurched into the wormhole, then hit a quantum brick wall of some sciencey stuff that spit them out in their mangled ship on Spintax, but over 8,000 years in the past.

They crashed into a forest, near the ancient pyramid and obelisk site that they had toured just a few days before. The Neighborly was totaled. It would never fly again. It was just dumb luck that the foursome survived at all, as badly damaged as the ship was. The banker had suffered an ugly bleeding gash across his whole face, cheek to cheek. Maxwell had a badly broken arm. They all four were bruised up head to toe, but they walked away from the crash alive, if not well.

They could see the tallest pyramid off in the distance. Having been there, and not knowing yet, that they were in the past, the four humans headed on foot towards the site, to find someone to help send them back home to Earth.

Unaccustomed to manual labor, and injured as they were, the four humans took most of the day with quite a lot of complaining to each other to arrive at the site. As the red dwarf sun was setting, they finally made it to where the Spintax International Archaeological Park's entrance was supposed to be. However, they found only a mud brick hut village surrounding the gold-covered temples. Maxwell might not have been a scientist, but he was smart, and he figured out right then, they were in the past.

"For the love of all that is holy!" Maxwell collapsed to the ground on his knees. "We've traveled back in their time. We are stranded here."

"Stranded. . . now." The banker cried, his tears mixing with the blood that dripped from the wound on his face.

The Spintaxian natives welcomed the humans again. The humans again couldn't fathom the financial system, as even then, 8,000 years in the past, the Spintaxians were already not using money or gold or any currency other than their compassionate system of rewarding everyone for how loved they were by others.

You'd not think four people could change a whole civilization, but these four humans were billionaires. They knew how to make others work to earn them obscene amounts of wealth, and how to make that wealth buy them power. Maxwell, the banker, and the real estate mogul were brilliant, if not in science, in finance. So that is what they did there on ancient Spintax. They grew huge amounts of wealth and power for each of the three of them just like they had done back on modern Earth, enabling them to buy their way to the new world to start with. The oil tycoon's heir had inherited his father's money but not his brilliance in finance, and didn't fare as well on ancient Spintax. He was spoiled and greedy but not gifted with the talents to make a fortune himself. Maxwell took pity on him though and kept him up as an advisor, once Maxwell had become King.

In eight thousand years, humans again discovered Spintax. Except this time when the billionaires stepped off the Neighborly they were met by a horde of twenty six Presidents and Kings and Prime Ministers from the twenty six wealthiest nations on Spintax, but none the leaders of the thirty four poor third world nations there. Then the humans were given a tour of the biggest factories by the corporation owners who were billionaires themselves despite no one loving them for their greedy selfish ways. Then they toured a gold mine under what had been the pyramids and obelisks site. They toured a debtors prison factory cranking out cheap clothing with the slave labor of the prisoners. They toured the King's palace, where they met Caregg, an administrative assistant to the King of that largest, most powerful nation on Spintax.

The two neighboring planets got along much better this time, understanding each other perfectly. The two planets became interstellar successful business allies, who made billions of billions of dollars mining, manufacturing, and building all over their little arm of the Milky Way galaxy. The four crewmen of the original Neighborly Earth spaceship would have been so proud had they seen how they did, after all, destroy the old Spintax.

###

About the Author

Ginger Strivelli is an artist and writer from Jupiter, North Carolina, who currently lives in Luxor, Egypt, with the youngest of her six children and several pets, including a baby camel.

Ginger writes both fiction and nonfiction, as well as some poetry. She writes often on the topics of her Pagan religion and on autism, as three of her six children are autistic. Ginger is a painter and enjoys many arts and crafts such as sewing and jewelry making. She also loves traveling and has visited India, Mexico, Belize, Greece, and other magical sites.

*****~~~~~*****

The Kromlau Gambit

by Steve Toase

The room was too hot and too small, and the black-haired man was coming up fast on the fly agaric he'd ingested in preparation for the meeting. Sand flies crawled across his scalp and over his eyebrows. He let them find the warmth of his mouth, dedicating each small death to a different perished god. Blood sacrifices were still blood sacrifices, no matter how small.

The door opened, and two men walked in, shadowed against the fluorescent lighting in the corridor beyond. The first, in his fifties and uniformed, stood to one side. Saluted. The second man sat down opposite, draping his white coat over the back of the chair. One hand went to the other wrist again and again, seeking out a patch of bloody and scabbed eczema. Soft skin trapped under the man's fingernails as he scratched.

"Thank you for joining us," the soldier said. "My name is General Vasiliev. I have oversight of this facility. Doctor Kuznetsov is our scientific director."

Finishing, he offered his hand. The black-haired man stared at the soft pink skin for a moment and ignored the gesture.

"I hope the journey from the airstrip wasn't too demanding," General Vasiliev continued.

The black-haired man smiled. Leaned back in his chair until it tipped onto two legs.

"The catering was lacking. I almost dined on the driver, until I realised there was no map in the vehicle for me to make my way here alone."

The two Russians looked at each other, unsure whether to laugh or not.

"And what should we call you?" Kuznetsov asked, nails still working a hole into his arm. The black-haired man licked his lips for a moment as he thought about the answer.

"You can call me Papa Yaga."

"Papa Yaga?" Annoyance shadowed Vasiliev's face as he spoke, and Papa Yaga smiled.

"It seems fitting, don't you think?"

"I do not," Kuznetsov said. "It seems like folklore and myth."

Papa Yaga stood and walked up to the large emblem that hung on the wall behind him.

"Do you know what they represent?"

"The hammer and the sickle?" the General said. Papa Yaga nodded. "The industrial worker and the peasant."

"And the red?"

"Socialism, of course," Kuznetsov interrupted.

Papa Yaga shook his head and ran a finger down the curved plaster blade, wincing as if it was freshly honed.

"The hammer is to represent those sacrificed to the three crippled gods. Their skulls crushed to spill their blood into packed dirt floors of ancient wooden temples."

General Vasiliev looked amused.

"And the sickle?"

"Those beheaded in the cornfields to bring a good harvest. If the edge was sharp, and the wound deep, the spine severed first time."

"And if not?"

Papa Yaga stared at Kuznetsov until the scientist looked away.

"A lot of peasant children grew up with the burbling of cut throats as their first lullaby." Opening a pocket, Papa Yaga took out a pipe, packed it with a selection of crushed leaves, and lit the mixture. "Would you like to know about the colour red?"

"Shall we get on with the reason we've convened here?" Kuznetsov said, standing and waiting for Vasiliev to join him. "Rather than getting distracted by this outdated superstition."

Papa Yaga smiled and held his arms wide, as if ready to embrace both his companions.

"Unfortunately for you, my man of science, outdated superstition is exactly why we're here. Did you manage to collect together the resources I requested?"

Kuznetsov opened the door.

"Please, follow us."

...

The hanger was vast. Corrugated ceilings held back tons of concrete and the desert sands beyond. They stood on a balcony overlooking the working floor, Papa Yaga between the General and the Scientist.

In the centre of the room a large crate waited unopened, surrounded by several smaller boxes.

"We have not begun processing the organic material. There was some uncertainty about whether you would require input at this stage."

Papa Yaga nodded, taking in the scene. Smiling to himself. His word had brought these rare artefacts across the globe to this Soviet facility in the Kazakhstan.

"Shall we go and inspect them?" he said.

...

Down on the working floor Vasiliev gestured for a soldier to come over with a crowbar. Papa Yaga took the tool, turned it over in his hand, and levered open the first crate.

"Just like Christmas," he said, shrugging when no one else smiled at his joke.

A scent like old wet leather spread around them. He reached inside and lifted out the piece of skin, running a finger across the tattooed elk antlers.

"The offering of human flesh," he said, showing it to the two Soviets. Handing the fragment to the waiting soldier, he opened the next crate, lifting out the tied bunches of herbs inside. Their fragrance did nothing to counter the reek of rotting meat spreading out across the hanger.

"Perfect. I like working with you gentlemen. You're very good at following orders. Now for the big one. If you wouldn't mind helping."

Kuznetsov clicked his fingers and several more troops came to stand around the large crate. One took the crowbar from Papa Yaga, working his way down each rough wooden panel, prising stamped designations apart as he opened the side.

The mammoth was upright and defrosting. Pools of dirty water collected in pale tubs underneath, placed there to stop leaks during transit. Papa Yaga took a small metal shot glass out of his jacket and dipped it in the melt-water, swallowing it in one.

"And the ancient mastodon for strength. If you can create a work party to clip the hair and remove the tusks, it will be much quicker than me attempting to do so by myself."

Kuznetsov nodded, and scribbled a note on a piece of paper.

"What about the meteor?" Vasiliev said, picking up the curved fragment of iron from the final crate.

"You had the metal prepared to my specifications?"

"Of course."

Papa Yaga sat cross legged on the floor, laying bunches of herbs out in a fan before him. The fly agaric was blossoming inside him now. Spreading mycelium through his veins. He exhaled and smiled.

"The meteor is a key."

"A key?"

"Quite literally a key. Over many centuries man has pigmented the earth with religion and magic and superstition. The taint of ritual has settled against the upper atmosphere, replicating a protective magical circle around the globe."

In the dust he drew a rough sphere, marking around the edge in symbols.

"This keeps out many, shall we say, problematic entities, but also prevents anything living escaping into the vastness and horror of the void."

"And the meteor can overcome this?"

"The meteor has entered our world from exactly that vastness and horror of the void. It will be recognised as it returns."

"Why do you need the rest of this?" Kuznetsov said.

"Everything needs a little ritual, Comrade, everything needs a little ritual. Now, if you don't mind, I wish to confirm my fee."

...

The cosmonaut sat alone in the sealed chamber, a book open on the desk in front of him. Papa Yaga tried to read the paragraphs, but the thick glass blurred the Cyrillic text.

"Senior Lieutenant Bragin. Awarded the Order of Alexander Nevsky, the Order of Glory Second Class, and The Order of Lenin."

"Fascinating. Will he be missed?"

Kuznetsov and Vasiliev looked to each other.

"Missed?" said the General.

"Does he have family?" Papa Yaga said.

Kuznetsov opened a file and searched for a piece of paper.

"Yes, a wife and two girls. Seven and Nine."

Papa Yaga nodded.

"Under ten but old enough to appreciate the loss of a parent. Their grief always tastes the sweetest. Why did you select him?"

"We have our own criteria, obviously. Competency as a pilot. Reactions in a crisis. Loyalty to the CCCP."

"No scandals? No whores or mistresses? No gambling debts or narcotics habits?"

"We were able to accommodate your requirements."

"You see, gentlemen. If we work together we can achieve great things. A pure soul is a delicate flavour. One to be savoured. Like fine caviar. Something I'm sure you gentlemen, as loyal party members, will be familiar with. A good untainted soul settles on one's tongue. Nip the edge with an incisor, and the flavour slides down one's throat."

Neither man looked at Papa Yaga, instead fixing their gaze on the small isolation cubicle where Senior Lieutenant Bragin continued to read his book.

"If you would be so kind as to take me back to the hangar, clear it of your men, and seal the doors against intrusions, I will prepare the materials. I'm so excited that I will play such an important role in the first living thing venturing beyond the planet."

General Vasiliev and Doctor Kuznetzov said nothing.

...

Alone in the vast hangar Papa Yaga chewed the final piece of fly agaric and opened his bag, taking out a knife, a glass vial, and a desiccated toad. The soldiers had piled the fibres of mammoth pelt beside the crate, arranging the tusks in a semi circle. With the knife in his right hand, he drew the flint blade across the palm of his left, then swapped it over, waiting until the blood seeped

34

from the cut into the handle. Once the connection was made and the white fibrous mycelium knitted themselves into the darkened wood, he started to carve the first piece of ivory.

The fragments fell away, until he held a single yellowed staff, carved over with forgotten letters. Depictions of flayed gods and hollowed out ghosts. Using the tip he pushed the fibres into a circle, placing inside the tattooed skin, a single pound of mammoth flesh, and the meteorite iron. Balancing the toad on top of the metal, Papa Yaga retreated beyond the circle, struck the flint blade against another fragment of iron, and started whispering an invocation as the mammoth fur ignited. The flames flared as his voice rose, jaw distending and tongue splitting to spatter words that shattered the microphones left in the hanger by his Soviet observers.

When he finished speaking, the flames extinguished themselves, and the blade tumbled from his hands. He walked across the circle of ash and picked up the dome-shaped fragment of meteor. The surface had melted and was now covered in twig-like symbols. Papa Yaga read them, ignoring the bulging in his peripheral vision as he did. Satisfied, he knocked on the hanger door and waited until he was let out. The guard tried to hide his fear at the blood dripping from Papa Yaga's eyes and as-yet-unhealed jaw.

...

"Install this piece of meteor in the space vessel's nose cone, and your cosmonaut will be the first living creature to bridge the gap between Earth and space."

"And our business is concluded?" asked Kuznetzov. His nails worried the scab on his arm once more. Blood dripped to clot a trail on the concrete.

"Once I collect my fee. I'll make all the arrangements for that. You just provide me with the launch time."

...

The scavenged electrical equipment looked out of place in the centre of the ritual. Tripod legs rested on the inner circle, each point marked with a precise sigil drawn in ash. Bones of the three sacred animals lay spread underneath, the vessel to hold the cosmonaut's soul balanced in the centre. The air smelt of solder and burnt wiring. Papa Yaga inhaled the fumes until they filled his lungs.

Leaning against the wall of the bunker, he waited for the launch. The monitoring devices crackled, empty of any signal. With his eyes closed he surveyed deeper levels.

When it came, the launch sent ripples through all the planes, corporeal and non-corporeal. Acoustic waves picked up by devices in the earth, and ethereal echoes from the extra charms he'd placed on the meteor iron. There were only ten minutes until the capsule reached space. Papa Yaga stood, stripped, and prepared himself.

Those ten minutes passed in a flurry of activity. Chants, invocations, and inhalations occupied his time. Then he waited. The primitive monitoring devices picked up the communications. He fitted the consumption mask to the vessel. Readied himself to feast.

Somewhere above him the first living creature to venture into space died, and his preparations snared the soul, funnelling it back to earth. He listened to it squirm and strain against the constraint of the fleshed tunnel that guided it through the atmosphere. Down into the small glass bowl. He checked the seal on his mask and waited.

The taste was the first sign something was wrong. The lack of delicacy. Of nuance. He recognised the flavour. Had consumed it in a more controlled manner many decades before.

Severed of flesh and earth, the dog's soul remembered. It remembered wolf and jackal. Becoming rage and anger, it remembered death carried in saucer eyes and cunning carried in seven tails. It remembered howling

36

the hunt while wearing clot red ears, and circling those found outside the boundary fence. And as it remembered, the dog's soul attacked every muscle, organ and ligament inside Papa Yaga.

Papa Yaga tried to prise himself away. The ritual was too far along. Claws and teeth still embedded in the soul tore at his throat and stomach in fear. Soon the organs and muscles inside his torso were little more than gristle. Now hollowed out, he recovered his balance and tore the mask from his face. He turned on the primitive radio in the corner of the room.

"The Union of Soviet Socialist Republics announces today to the world that it has successfully sent the first living creature into orbit. At 5:30 pm Moscow time, a craft was launched with a dog as a passenger to test the viability of manned spaceflight. In light of the huge advances represented by this successful mission the Union of Soviet Socialist Republics will continue with its space programme and maintain its position as the world leader in off-planet exploration."

Curled on the floor Papa Yaga waited until the last of the animal's soul dissolved and as it faded to aftertaste on his tongue he screamed until the concrete around him cracked in two.

About the Author

Steve Toase's fiction has appeared in *Aurealis, Not One Of Us, Pantheon Magazine,* and *Tales To Terrify* podcast, among others. His story, "Call Out" (first published in *Innsmouth Magazine*) was reprinted in *The Best Horror Of The Year 6*, and "Fate's Mask" was mentioned in the summation. Steve writes regularly for *Fortean Times*; his article was the cover story of FT358.

*****~~~~~*****

Vincenzo, the Starry Messenger

by Dr. Jackie Ferris

Florence, 22 June 1633

Vincenzo tiptoed into the workshop. The faint glow of moonlight offered little illumination, but lighting a candle increased the risk of being seen. Earlier that evening the guards had left with most of Galileo's possessions. Tomorrow they would return to take the telescope or destroy it, but tonight it stood like a sentinel staring into the darkness, daring him to use it.

He glanced at the book discarded on the desk; its title: *Dialogue Concerning the Two Chief World Systems* had resulted in his master's imprisonment for heresy. He grimaced; if the book had sealed Galileo's demise, the telescope had prompted it. The planets revolving around the sun were easily identifiable through its refractory lens. Galileo called the telescope "the starry messenger"—for the Church it was the harbinger of doom. The coffee houses of Florence and Rome were rampant with discussions of what the Earth revolving around the Sun meant. The idea had been made moot by Copernicus almost a hundred years earlier with barely a ripple of concern. Unlike his predecessor, Galileo had openly defied the Church with the publication of his sacrilegious book. It questioned the relevance and existence of God—the earth's creator—if the earth was not the centre of everything. The Church had no desire to pose the question, never mind answer it, but every learned person was asking where or if God fitted into Galileo's new world order.

The telescope was the key into a planetary system that changed everything. Tomorrow it would be smashed; the guards had already destroyed nearly a hundred others. This one was the first to glimpse Jupiter's moons. Vincenzo sighed—it was an entrance into worlds that until now he had only plotted on the planetary charts.

He crept closer and then stopped to look down at the Ponte Vecchio. Once, butchers had sold their meat there; it was a meeting place for people who couldn't afford the coffee houses. That stopped when the Medicis commissioned a passageway above it. Now the shops were the exclusive domain of goldsmiths. The Medicis couldn't stand the smell of rotten meat, yet the events of the last few months proved that Galileo was as much a victim of their whims as the butchers. It was their power and need to dominate that pulled the Pope's strings. Religion was synonymous with power—the Medicis needed the Pope to front their schemes just like they needed the goldsmiths to consolidate their show of wealth.

Turning away from the window, he studied the telescope. It was like a stick insect perched on a stand. Vincenzo inched closer and threw his long brown locks over his shoulder as he pressed his eye closer to the telescope. He gasped; just as Galileo had said, the planet Jupiter stared back at him. Beyond Jupiter he glimpsed a twinkling light, one of Jupiter's four moons. The narrow range of the telescope meant it was little larger than a pinprick, but it was visible. He peered further into the telescope, hoping that the closer he got the more he could see. In that instant everything blurred.

He grabbed the scope and tugged, it but his eye was jammed tight. Finally, with an almighty heave he pulled away.

Vincenzo staggered—everything was black. It was freezing. He pulled his lucco tighter around him but his cloak was scarce protection from the bitter cold. The desk and telescope had vanished.

"Where am I?" The question erupted from his panic. "I can't see."

"Eyes are blinded in an icy sea."

Vincenzo laughed nervously as he tried to peer through the icy fog. "This is Florence, there are no icy seas."

"Your consciousness has left that space—you have no need of eyes. Galileo called this one of Jupiter's moons. It has oxygen—you can breathe."

Vincenzo breathed in deeply. "I'm dreaming."

"Dreams are mind cascades—this isn't a dream."

"You're nothing more than a voice in an icy fog. It must be a dream." Vincenzo's words resounded off the ice.

"Your conclusion betrays your inability to understand me. Allow me to pose the same question to you. Who are you?"

"That's easy, I am Vincenzo." His words echoed around the ice, taunting him.

"A name is a label; your answer defines your ineptitude."

"Ineptitude?" Vincenzo had a horrible feeling whoever had spoken was right.

"According to humans, God created your earth—he made it and will destroy it. Galileo has proved that definition is ill-judged. You are caught within the confines of a human-box."

"Human-box?"

"Your sounds are based on what you hear, your vision on what you see. There are more things in the universes than can be seen or heard. Matter is a physical persona—the universe is composed of more than matter."

"Then what are you?"

"I am you in a different form—everything in our universes is connected. Here, on the moon you will know as Ganymede, we exist in a more advanced state than human."

Vincenzo shook his long locks. "That's ridiculous, how can you be superior to me?"

"You betray your origins. I did not claim superiority, only advancement. The Church demanded superiority on the basis of God. Now you do the same because you are human. You are obsessed with classification, not form."

"I can't even see you. Is this a weird dream, or am I crazy with fear?"

"It's not a dream; it's a human out-of-body experience. You define and describe everything in the physical form of matter. Matter is a base form of existence. We don't depend on it here."

"Then why did you say that we are connected?"

"Everything in the universes is related. The human problem is that you are constrained by the human-box of God. You created God to explain your beginnings, but you insist that God created you. Galileo revealed that the Earth is not the centre of the universe; what he couldn't know is that what you see is a small part of what is really there. His telescope shows only a fragment of the heavens. There's darkness out there, yet you ignore it."

"Why should I listen to you? I don't even know how I got here."

"You're out of the human-box. I sucked you through the telescope into what you term my brain, although it's really my consciousness."

Vincenzo shook his head. "Impossible; perhaps I was knocked out by one of the guards."

"Does this look like a jail?"

"Not exactly."

A piece of ice dropped onto Vincenzo's foot.

"Pick it up."

Vincenzo bent down. The ice should have felt cold, but it didn't. He cradled it in the palm of his hand.

"What can you see?" the voice demanded.

"Nothing."

"No-thing or no-think, that's your future; in your human future, machines will take over. In a millennium, they will outgrow you. Even then, because machines are formed from matter, they will never have a pure intelligence. Life on Earth is constrained by the human-box of matter; it's time you stared into the darkness. God, aka the Church, made you afraid of the dark—it's how the Church controlled you.

"Lift your thoughts beyond what you think you know. God has lost its purpose. More importantly, matter is redundant—like God, it restrains your thought processes; the physical world is immaterial in the scheme of things. When you gaze into the heavens, explore the darkness not the stars. You, Vincenzo, can be the Earth's starry messenger and transcend matter. When I return you to your world, think about it."

Vincenzo was about to retort, when everything turned black. He staggered and then opened his eyes. He was back in the room with Galileo's telescope. He felt the piercing cold in his palm—it was the crystal of ice.

It was the beginning of summer, so it was impossible to have an ice chunk in his hand. Seconds later the Medici guards stormed in.

"We believe you have the telescope—it's a threat against God."

The ice burning in Vincenzo's hand gave him confidence. "And if God does not exist?"

"Then you must spend hell in prison."

"It matters not."

"Then you have never been imprisoned. The cell will bring you to your senses."

"It matters not, because matter does not matter."

"You're bewitched."

Vincenzo smiled. "Prison, like the human-box, constrains us because of the limitations we place on ourselves. The future will prove it, because you will not silence me or my master. We must look beyond ourselves and into the darkness for the truth. Matter is a base form; we will transcend our human box—the heavens are nothing like we think they are. Do not be confused, the answer does not lie in matter or even dark matter—the answer lies in darkness. Others who come after me will know that I am the starry messenger."

About the Author

Dr. Jackie Ferris is a traveler and writer interested in history and the future, a woman who likes to do things her way and enjoys new adventures.

Her background is in mental health and community programmes across Europe as well as producing educational booklets.

*****~~~*****

A Hard-Fought Episode at the TON-1 Black Hole

by Eric J. Guignard

It was half past that time of night when most sensible beings did their sleeping, but the freighter port of Mos Don never was sensible—it never shut down, never slept, never stopped carousing or fighting or depraving. And now it was burning, so it was worse. But still it did not stop in any of its ways.

The long haul driver pilot Milky Blue had parked his Peterbilt Space-5500 rig for a load-in at Jinn Wo's Export and Distribution. Every dock and bay of the superstructure was packed, with a line of other tractor shuttles a dozen deep waiting their turn to pull in next.

Lines were longest at Jinn Wo's, for she paid the best. The port was burning slow, and only getting worse, and the rush and the shoving and the evacuation efforts for all of it were massive. No one wanted to leave property behind if time remained to get it out, and every long hauler in the galaxy had made their way here for an easy paycheck.

Load-Bots had long since short-circuited from the radiating gamma rays that swept the port every ten minutes, so freight had to be loaded in the way of the ancients—by hand. Every other dock had roughneck bruisers tossin' in crates and furniture faster than warp simulators, but the only hands that loaded freight into Milky's trailer were tender and slow-moving, the suction grips of three expressionless Albore-5 starlings picked by Jinn herself. Jinn was taking no chances with *this* cargo.

"You know what this means to me, *seh*?" she asked.

"I do," Milky answered. Milky had a face like the ass end of a dak-yak and a matching stubborn streak to boot. He was unapologetic for both.

They walked down the warehouse corridor against a mass of humans, aliens, and other amorphid drivers who were bustling and shouting from dock to dock. There were towering bowl-headed Kes-3K mechanics and slithering Tarkaaan convoy pilots, a group of half-humans arguing Union politics, and gear-shift jockeys from Puppis White and GH-Gorn and a hundred other planets Milky had flown to.

"Gentle, but fast," Jinn reminded him, her green skin seeming to flutter like wind-swept leaves as she spoke. "This cargo is most priceless to me. Must arrive in two weeks. No side-trips, no stops even. No problem for you, *seh*?"

The crowds around them got tighter. Shouts, orders, curses, all in a melee of competing voices and alien babble. It reminded Milky of the fleshmongers on market day at Libra Libra. One of the GH-Gorn drivers had paused beside them, seeming to wait for an opening to pass through the lines.

"You know me," Milky said. "I got a sleeper cab and purpose, not to mention a pretty lil' co-pilot who doesn't ever rest."

He put his arm around the dark-haired female at his side. She was dressed in fringe and spangle and wore a Stetson hat on her head that doubled as a space helmet at the touch of a button. "This is Patsy. Patsy, Jinn is the bona-fide queen of verdant life. She knows it all and has it all."

A Hard-Fought Episode

"Right nice to meet you, ma'am," Patsy said. "You know what they say: Any friend of Milky's is. . . well, someone who I got to question their judgment."

"Hey now!" Milky chuckled, giving her a playful elbow in the side, beneath her six-gun shoulder holster. She was the only one who could bring that rare smile to his face.

A long snake's tongue flicked out from Jinn's mouth as she looked thoughtfully at Patsy. "I thought they banned A.I. to replicate life."

"She was made before all that legislative nonsense," Milky said and winked. "Not like *you* worry much about regulations anyway."

Jinn's tongue vanished back in her mouth as she smiled coyly. Only the points of dual fangs remained visible.

Milky added, "I rescued her from a slag pit on Festoon 8. Originally she comes from my part of the universe, this reproduced singer from a few millennia ago, name of Patsy Cline."

Patsy clutched her hip. "And I feel every one of those millennia in my circuitry."

An explosion rocked the warehouse. Milky stumbled. Jinn cursed. Shouts went up from the throngs of truckers and workers rushing around them.

"The building's hydrogen tanks are overheating. You must hurry," Jinn said.

"It's only getting worse, ain't it?" Patsy asked. "Just like always."

"Two days more," Jinn answered.

"*Light* days," Milky corrected. "Right?"

"Technicalities. . . we'll be rubble by then anyway. It's the gamma rays, pounding us like earthquake tremors. They're relentless, getting stronger."

"Never could've imagined anything like this," Milky muttered. "It's one thing to have two black holes

47

colliding, but this is the damnedest phenomenon of odds. . . you got *four* black holes all joining at the same time."

"They're calling it TON-1. It'll be the single greatest black hole in all of existence," Patsy said.

"*Seh*, and if you're not gone soon, you'll be part of it."

Milky felt a tingle, like something settling on his shoulder, and he turned just enough to glance back through the corner of his eye. The driver he'd noticed earlier from GH-Gorn was pacing them, mouthing into a transponder and looking occupied, but with his ear turned their way. Something about him was familiar, and not in a good way.

"Starlings are done loading," Jinn said, tapping a button on her wrist console. "Now you fly."

Milky nodded and dropped a four-inch shiv into his palm. He rounded suddenly, ready to confront the eavesdropper, but the driver had vanished into the crowd. Milky curled a lip thoughtfully.

...

Two hours and a ream of flight documents later, Milky patted the double tungsten locks that latched the semi-trailer's doors. His rig was thirty years old, though it showed those years tenfold. If her dents could talk, Milky liked to say, your ears would give out before you got to the fifth vacuum coupling.

He flew an eighteen-wheeler, where the wheels had been replaced by Vertical-Lateral Thrusters the size of asteroids, each lowered far below the wheel wells. Though they'd been modified for maximum fusion-driven flight, Milky had no delusions that he was the fastest, but his rig's strength was in endurance; when flashier tractors burned out, his hadn't even gone into overdrive. The cab was gunmetal gray, smashed in on every corner with more scratches and dings than a flame rock shower, and the trailer's 52-foot carbon-shelled length was topped by articulated rudder fins.

A Hard-Fought Episode

There wasn't much else that Milky cared for in the universe but what he had before him: his rig and Patsy Cline.

"The colliding black holes," Patsy said. "They're expelling mass in gravitational waves."

"Yeah, I know, and shootin' out fragments and gamma bursts and shit," Milky said.

"No, I mean, I *feel* the waves, darlin', rolling through every few minutes. My sensors, we're being slightly compressed in width and stretched in height, just a shift of a millimeter, then returned to normal, but it's getting stronger."

"We'll be fine inside the cab. Artificial gravity controls will keep us stable, so let's get haulin'."

Milky buckled into the driver's seat, and Patsy into the gunner's. Between them were about twenty video screens and a hundred buttons and levers and dials, targeting arrays, launchers, and a cigarette lighter. A scanner transceiver ran across the dash, and warmers glowed crimson red. A horseshoe air freshener hung from the rearview mirror.

The long-barreled gear shift had a Solar Ball knob top; Milky put one hand over it and Patsy a hand over his.

"I love this part," she said, "leavin' for the open road." She started singing one of Milky's favorite tunes, a verse about being *back in baby's arms*.

The bay doors opened, and they flew out into space.

"Keep up that pretty voice, and two weeks will go by in a snap," Milky said. "We got a direct path for Polypody-E3, Fern World."

"*Direct* would take you right into TON-1, darlin'. I don't want to be a singularity anytime soon."

"A figure of speech. We'll skirt the curve of its event horizon rather than fly all the way around."

"So long as 'skirt' means keeping a far distance away."

"But it's a mighty scenic view close in."

Her eyes sparkled as she rolled them. "A view into nothingness."

"At least there's no other traffic out here."

"I'd guess it's something to do with the propensity of other pilots to avoid black holes rather than fly closer in."

"Smartass."

They turned to look upon the merging black holes in the distance, all four in various sizes and stages of seeming to eat each other up. It was like swirling a giant brush of black paint over a canvas of stars. Just empty holes of existence surrounded by astral debris and pale reddish clouds. A violent jet of gas suddenly shot out, looking like a monstrous death ray.

He turned his steering wheel left to fly outside its radius, and looked in the sideview mirror. "Cancel that, Patsy, we're not alone."

She adjusted her own mirror. "What are those, astrocycles?"

"Don't look like they're avoiding TON-1 either, and they're comin' in fast."

"Maybe they know something we don't, a better way around?"

Milky gritted his teeth. "They're flyin' in dark."

"What's that mean?"

"I think it means they're set on raiding us."

Patsy didn't waste a moment but primed the roof-mounted double-barreled QF Plasma gun. Then she armed the undercarriage belly tracking-gun. "They must've followed from Jinn's. But why us? I thought the other freighters are the ones carrying her loot."

"Damn it all, I should've recognized him earlier," Milky said. "I caught one of the other drivers listening in on Jinn when she was talking to us. He must've heard her say how this cargo was *priceless*, probably thought to cash in on a well-timed opportunity. That driver was from GH-

Gorn, I could tell the way his elbow was double-jointed when holding up his transponder, and his nose was nothing but a pair of slits. I remember him now from an OrbitComm report, a *Wanted* notice."

"Wanted for real bad things, I'm guessing, if he made it to OrbitComm desks."

"He's leader of a gang, six of 'em that knock over long haul trucks, steal the cargo *and* the truck, leave the driver floatin' away in the vacuum of doomsday. One driver's spacesuit and oxygen held long enough that he was picked up by a recon shuttle, so he gave the details and description of the heist. Justice agents figured out real quick who the gang leader was, name of Raid-Calipso, an astro biker who broke out of hyper lock-up two years ago. No knowing, either, how often he's done this before. Long haulers go missing all the time. . . though we ain't much *missed*, if you know what I mean."

"I'll sing you a real sad blues song about that another time, darlin'," Patsy said. "But what are we going to do now?"

Milky thought hard and fast, and he veered back to the right, barreling once again toward the black hole. He counted all six bikers in the mirror, three on each side, the lead pair closing in only several dozen kilometers back. No way he could outrun 'em; astrocycles were sleek one-man pods with short clutch wings and spinning booster rockets behind the hugger. They were fast.

Milky's Comm Drive video screen flashed on.

It was Raid-Calipso, smiling, like he'd just shared a joke. "Hey, friend." His voice was an electronic translation, coming from the chip under his pale tongue. "Your tail light's out. Whyn't you pull over, we'll give you a hand to fix it."

"It's all right," Milky replied. "I don't plan on braking anytime soon."

Raid didn't stop smiling. "Well then, I'll give it to you straight. We want what you got in that trailer."

"You can suck a turd-toad's ass before I give it up to you."

Now Raid's smile went away. "You got one chance to pull over, and we'll let you go unharmed. Otherwise, the last few minutes of your life are gonna end up in a lot of screaming and bleeding."

Milky scoffed. "Here's my counter-offer."

Patsy blew a kiss at the screen and pulled a trigger. Streaks of light blasted out from the undercarriage gun and one of the lead cycles burst into a fireball of shrapnel and alien flesh.

Raid's face turned livid, and the Comm Drive screen flashed off.

Then all hell broke loose. The astrocycles spread out, returning fire, and plasma bolts punished the back of Milky's rig. The glow of molten metal surrounded his rear vid screens while something snapped off his fenders and his mud flaps disintegrated. One of his Vertical-Lateral Thrusters detonated into a geyser of debris. Milky felt his rig pull hard downward, and Patsy's next shots went wild. He vaguely realized how close he was getting to the edge of the black hole's event horizon, feeling the gravitational pull on his tractor shuttle getting stronger and stronger, which he thought he could use to his advantage.

He steered hard into the downward skid, letting the extra gravitational pull accelerate the movement, which whipped them around into a steep curve. It was a wild, dangerous maneuver, as the trailer could lock up against the hitch and send his whole rig into an uncontrollable roll straight into TON-1, but it held, and he wheeled back to face the bikers head-on.

They weren't expecting that.

Milky always believed in a good bullbar, the type of a metal grill guard used to protect the front bumper of a cab from collision, or to push aside floating space junk, or—in this case—to obliterate an oncoming biker.

A Hard-Fought Episode

The nearest astrocycle smashed dead-center into it, splattering like a bug on a windshield.

"Nice driving," Patsy said as she swiveled the roof-mounted QF Plasma gun. A targeting light blinked green, and she triggered a shot, and another astrocycle fell away like a fiery comet.

"Nice shootin'," Milky answered.

He revved up and pulled forward, and a biker flew underneath and blasted upward, raking the undercarriage on the trailer with his salvo. Red lights flashed, and sirens blared across Milky's console.

"Damn, chassis has been compromised, we've lost targeting!"

"Belly gun's out," Patsy said.

Milky spun the wheel back around, and he pulled again toward the event horizon, skimming along its greatest pull.

Once inside, nothing escapes black holes, not even light. . . *most of the time.* But the magnitude of the four colliding black holes was so great that even *it* had to release extra mass that was being displaced in the universe, resulting in outward gravitational waves and gamma rays and releasing jets of ionized gas. Milky had seen it earlier in the flight, the death-ray look of a jet that began within a sudden swirling reddish cloud.

He saw a cloud forming now and flew straight at it. The remaining astrocycles followed, staying underneath him, where his damaged gun couldn't fire. The bikers blasted again, and a second of his thrusters ruptured.

The gas cloud ahead began to glow bright as a miniature sun, and, at the last, Milky pulled hard away, jackknifing to the left, just as a release of gas jetted out like a geyser. The jet engulfed one of the bikers, and he and his cycle vanished.

Milky went hand-over-hand, pulling back out of the gravitational pull. There were two astrocycles left.

"By the way, what's so *priceless* about Jinn's cargo?" Patsy asked, scanning all the video screens. "I thought there wasn't anything left in the universe worth more than goldonium chips, and I know we're not lugging those."

A sensor went off as something landed on the trailer's back door. Milky cursed. A vid screen showed one of the bikers had tethered himself to the back of the trailer. His cycle was moored to the side as tight as a starling's suction-grip. Attached as the biker was, there was no way to shake him loose.

"It's Jinn's brood," Milky replied to Patsy.

"*Brood,* as in children? Why are they in a cargo trailer, not flying in a transport?"

The bright flare of an astro-torch lit up the rear vid screen. The biker started cutting through the door locks.

"They're offspring, but not exactly children. More of. . . plant people." Milky dropped the rig into a deep dive, then soared and turned up. Still the biker clung on. The first lock fell apart, and the second was half-severed. "See, interstellar law banned breeding with plant life, so with Mos Don orbiting into TON-1, Jinn had to evacuate her progeny clandestinely."

"Breeding with plant life! How!?"

The second lock fell away. The trailer doors swung open.

"Like I said earlier, Jinn is the queen of verdant life, meaning in the way of an insect queen. Her brood are half-animate, half-plant. You know what a Venus flytrap is?"

"Sure," Patsy said. "Had them back home when I was a girl in Virginia."

The biker pulled himself inside.

"Imagine those," Milky said. "But a lot larger. And intelligent. And generally pissed-off."

Though sound can't be heard in space, Milky imagined he heard a sudden and long-drawn out scream.

Then a space boot with a chewed-off foot floated out from the trailer's back. A bloody helmet followed.

"Starlings did a good job securing the cargo at least. *They* won't fall out."

"Good thing," Milky said, "since we got one biker left."

The last astrocycle sideswiped the truck's cab, and its rider fired a laser pistol at Milky's driver's side window. The micro-silicate glass held.

"Got those reinforced three years ago, asshole," Milky muttered, and steered hard to slam back against the cycle. A clutch wing crumpled against the rig's front wheel well and the metal entanglement locked the two craft together. The rider leapt off, rolling over to land on Milky's hood.

The rider's spacesuit was covered in patches of skulls and flaming swords, and his helmet had spikes coming out like an armored mace. He turned his head up to look right at them as Milky's Comm Drive video screen flashed back on.

It was Raid-Calipso, smiling again. "You're dead, trucker." He held on with his fingers sunk deep into a ventilation port on the hood, while his other hand pulled out a thermite grenade from his chest bandolier.

"He's too close in, out of range of the roof gun!" Patsy shouted. "Can you shake him off?"

"He's double-jointed, can hold on like a spidersaur," Milky said grimly. As close as Raid was, Milky knew that grenade would incinerate the front of the cab, melt everything inside, him and Patsy both. Raid might even escape if the blast freed his bike.

Milky had an idea.

He floored the accelerator, aiming straight toward the black holes.

"Looks like you got my crew, trucker," Raid said, "but I'll get the last laugh." He raised the grenade.

Gravity-drive sensors rang on high alert, and Milky's rig started shuddering.

"Wait," Milky told Raid. "I surrender."

He braked evenly, and hit reverse thrusters to counter the suction pull of Ton-1. Something inside the engine squealed, straining.

"What?!" Patsy yelled "Are you out of your mind?"

Raid's smile got bigger. "You got brains after all. Open your door."

They were already on the verge of falling through the event horizon, the point of no longer being able to fight against the black hole's gravitational pull, and his truck was shuddering like it was getting wrenched apart at the seams, but it endured. The pressure on Raid must be immense, yet the alien was still holding too. Where was *his* point of no return?

Milky had remembered Patsy describing the feeling in Mos Don bay of the gravity waves rolling through every few minutes, like ocean waves, compressing and stretching everything infinitesimally. Only out here, closer in, the effect would be amplified immensely—and that's when the next wave rolled in.

The truck and trailer were angled straight in, but, with its length, its center of mass was much farther back than Raid's body center. Milky popped the clutch and levered into reverse while the extra gravitational pull on Raid's feet from the colliding black holes took him like a clamp.

The biker's face froze, then contorted into a look of sheer terror. He dropped the grenade and sunk both hands into the ventilation ports, but he didn't have a chance. He shrieked just before the Comm Drive screen flashed off. Milky backed out as fast as he could, and Raid was pulled away into the black holes, where he appeared frozen on its edge, slowly expanding out, flattening and spreading like a dissipating cloud.

"His last laugh didn't sound so funny after all," Patsy said.

"You know," Milky said. "You come out here a thousand years from now, long after I'm gone, and you'll still see Raid stuck like that, stretching forever in spacetime. It's like a photograph in the stars just for you, pretty lady. Something to remember our times together." He winked at her.

"You're a real Don Juan, Milky."

"That and hazard pay oughta cover this rig's repairs."

And with that, he turned the truck away from one horizon and aimed for another, the faraway edge of Fern World.

About the Author

Eric Guignard's stories and nonfiction have appeared in publications such as *Nightmare Magazine*, *Black Static*, *Gamut*, *Shock Totem*, *Buzzy Magazine*, and *Dark Discoveries Magazine*, as well as the Third Flatiron anthology, *Ain't Superstitious.*

*****~~~~~*****

Titan Is All the Rage

by Jemima Pett

"I'm bored."

"You're always bored."

"We're always going to the same places, that's why."

Sand-yachting on Mars had become tedious, and snowboarding on the polar ice caps had given Kent and me a few week's respite, until the ennui set in again.

"I have to go back to the corporation in ten days," I told him. "Do you want to stay here or go back to Earth for the rest of the time?"

If we went back he could crow about it sooner for longer. If we stayed for more snowboarding, or returned to sand-yachting, or even switched to float-rapids down the dusty canyons, he'd build up new stories to keep him one-up in the adventure stakes.

"Let's go up to Poris Major and try some canyoning."

Good. It kept me out of instant communication range for longer. Besides, I had a marketing idea that I wanted to work on undisturbed.

Had the guys on Titan got far enough to open up the oceans for tourism? They were definitely close; the corporation had funded the exploration, and realising our investment was my priority. My last exchange with them indicated possibilities for plume-shooting, dune-buggies,

59

and cryo-diving, as well as submarine wildlife tours. I grabbed my tab and sketched out a plume-shooting storyboard, while Kent got another round of drinks.

...

Twenty-three months later I was on the third trip with Satvitours. My marketing campaign had hit the Mons Carlo set at exactly the right time: the destruction of the entire fleet during the trans-Pacific Air Trophy had them looking for new pastimes. Submarine tours were the ground-breakers, being the least risky. Our SS Nefertiti was exactly what the rich and indolent wanted. We'd even secured the services of Guilie Attenborough-Grylls as the resident expert to add the extra cachet this class required.

I'd been through the report from the first trip, making sure it was fully sanitised before leaking it to the press; the initial hitches had been smoothed out in time for the second. Only minor inconveniences had irritated the pioneers on that one. They'd been well paid to sing its praises, and with the inclusion of Paul Andray on the guest list, we had global coverage. Eleven couples were the paying complement this sailing, each fully pampered by the twenty-four crew, plus Captain Jennings and his Number Two, Markside.

As soon as the passengers awoke from their transit-sleep, we held a reorientation programme in the dining room. Our first priority was to remind them they were on a space ship and re-establish the rules and safety procedures. After breakfast, we taught them the basics of Titan—since none of them would have done any homework beforehand. That could be lethal, as our one-time competitors had found when one of their celebrity customers completely forgot that Mars did not have an Earth atmosphere, and had gone outside unsuited.

So, once they had understood that the atmosphere at the surface was poisonous—at 95% nitrogen, 5% methane—and cold (minus 180 degreesC), all we had to do was show them how the cocoons worked, how they could view the surface features, the different light effects possible for their digiscopes, and where to look for the effect of Saturn above the clouds. Then we reminded them of the itinerary. Day one: surface viewing and tour of the village. Flight to the Ontario Lake with the opportunity for touch-down at the Equator and viewing the dune system. Dinner on board before arriving at Ontario and boarding the SS Nefertiti.

"Why don't we land at the Nefertiti straight away?" a large man in multicoloured robes dripping with gold jewellery asked.

"That was in your booking information pack." Karal, our rep, was programmed for patience. "The village gives you the proper Titan bio-adjustment, and you get to see the highlights of the surface before we submerge and take the passage through the crust." He described the rest of the trip: four days on the Nefertiti, with lectures from Guilie, which could be accessed at any time post-departure. Guilie would also attend the four viewing areas to discuss any wildlife sightings.

"If you see something and I'm not there, just buzz and I'll come, or I'll check on the video with you so that I don't miss it." Guilie was the world's expert on Titan's oceanographic life. We could use the word expert, because nobody else knew anything. Guilie received regular updates from the scientists.

"This lot are so boring," Kent said as we took our private seats for landing.

"This lot are paying, and will boast to their friends."

...

Titan was all I had hoped. Three days of minimalist architecture, safety suits at all times, and gawping at the sights. At first, looking out on what Arthur Conan Doyle described as a "London Peculiar" for eighteen hours until sleep beckoned sounds mind-numbing.

In fact the mist swirled and shifted, revealing tantalising glimpses of ice features. Ideas roiled in my brain. Ice-skating on Titan—who could resist it? Hockey tournaments, maybe? When we reached Lake Ontario the atmosphere was thinner, and we could see stars through gaps in the clouds. This part of the sky was hardly affected by Saturn at all, and we got a fleeting glimpse of Hyperion, the next moon outwards.

The viewing areas of the Nefertiti contained sufficient reference stations to occupy everyone while waiting for something to happen outside. Guilie worked overtime, using the screen to pick out the microscopic life identified so far.

"Even this place is boring," Kent complained on our third night.

The fourth day was not boring.

At breakfast Commander Markside addressed us. "We are approaching a turbulent area of the ocean. Please use your safety straps at all times, especially when moving around. You can be thrown from your feet, or even from your seat, before we have time to press the alert button. It is totally unpredictable. I don't want you to be injured, so you must do as I say."

The way he said that made me wonder. Nobody wanted anyone to be injured. We wouldn't run the trip if there was serious risk of injury. Weren't we avoiding the turbulent areas?

I waited till everyone was on their way to the viewing areas. Everyone caught their safety straps onto the overhead rail, and managed them without too much entanglement. I slipped off to the ship's control room.

"What do you mean by turbulence?" I asked, after exchanging pleasantries.

I was answered by a lurch to the left, which threw me to the right. The harness reeled in the slack of the safety line automatically, and I was jerked upwards before I could collide with anything. Captain Jennings was in full harness in his seat, slapping controls and barking orders in a language I didn't understand. He was getting responses from Markside and the other crewmember, whose face was drained of blood. The Nefertiti gained her elegant balance again, and he turned to me.

"Sorry, ma'am; that was turbulence. There'll be more."

"But I thought. . . "

"So did we. This is not supposed to be an active area. The readings we had earlier suggest there's a plume building somewhere nearby, but we don't know where it'll erupt."

"A plume—you mean for plume-shooting?"

He grinned, not smiling. "Plume shooting, yes, you could say that—Saturn's rings, Mark, what's that?" His face changed completely as something loomed in their forward screen. "Guilie, large C1 in forward zone, going left!"

I couldn't see what he was looking at and by the time I'd found it, there was just a wake in the hydrocarbon soup outside.

"Should we take our safety seats, do you think?" I asked.

"I don't want to upset the tourists, but yes. Don't alarm them."

"They're probably alarmed already."

He slapped the ship-wide comms again. "Sorry about that, ladies and gentlemen. Welcome to Titan's seas. We've found a nice area of turbulence previously unmapped, so think of yourselves as pioneers. Your personal crewmember will be with you shortly to escort you to your safety seat. They will remain with you at this time; please follow their instructions promptly and without drama. Your screens will continue to show you anything of interest."

"'Remaining with us' is code for emergency drill, isn't it?"

He studied me, gauging my propensity to hysteria. "Yes," he replied. "What do you know of plume-riding, anyway?"

"I've been plume-shooting in Iceland, and in Indonesia," I said tentatively. I loved drawing it but I hated doing it. My crewmember appeared by my side.

"Do you want to do it here, or with your partner?"

"Do I get to know what's going on if I stay here?"

"Yes, you only get the sanitised version with the others. Oh—JUMP SEATS!"

He yelled the last words, presumably over the comms too, and my crewmember dragged me into a safety seat, thumped the auto-restraints and thumped her own as she sat in the one adjacent.

I had no time to complain as the world spun my stomach around my ears, my eyeballs pressed against my skull, and my nose started bleeding. I didn't lose my breakfast, but my suit took a big dump into its waste area. The G-force pressed me to the seat as I crashed into it, and I thought my hip joint would dislocate. If I thought anything at all, that is—maybe I realised that when I relived the whole thing later. I think I heard Jennings giving orders, and Markside calling out decreasing numbers. I remember someone swearing and saying he hoped the crust had blown. I had my eyes screwed tight shut, so I didn't respond to the cry, "Look at that mother!" or the whoops that sounded afterwards.

The noise was incredible. Banging and crashing, and swooshing, and bangs which made the hull ring, and pushed us from side to side. I think we were pointed upwards, the way we were being thrown. I asked afterwards, and Markside said the safety seats automatically orientate themselves to support us against G-forces. Some of the banging was hydrocarbon ice, some was shattered crust. Then it all became quiet, the G-forces diminished, and we were weightless. I opened my eyes. Sore, a bit blurry, but okay.

"Top of the curve," said Jennings. "Crewmembers report by number."

I could hear the crewmembers report in, repeating a number and "AOK" till my crewmember said, "Twenty-four, AOK," and I saw Jennings's shoulders relax.

"Well, ladies and gentlemen, congratulations. You are the first tourists to experience a Titan plume. I hope you enjoyed it, and I apologise we weren't able to give you a preparatory briefing. I was expecting to do that tomorrow. Markside will give you a rerun of it, just explaining what happened, and showing you what you missed, later this evening. We are now in free fall, and will shortly regain gravity. Ah, here it comes now. I will deploy our balloon chutes when we reach the right altitude, and we will land in the vicinity of Cassini station."

He didn't say then that we would miss the last day of our cruise, but everyone was more than happy to regain the cramped safety of the station. We worked out what had happened, recorded our experiences, turned it into a fantastic experience, and remembered to view the record of the whale-like jellyfish creature that had escaped the plume as we entered it.

The buzz we created meant that Titan is all the rage now, although nobody on that tour is going back. Not even snowboarding on Mars holds any interest. Kent is never bored. I only work when I want to. Give me a book, a pool and a waiter, somewhere on an island on Earth, and I'm happy.

###

About the Author

Since rediscovering her fiction mojo, Jemima Pett has thrown aside academic science papers and delved into the world of fantasy, time travel, and space opera. Her first foray into juvenile fiction was a simple trilogy: two princelings solved time tunnel twists, pirate predations, and revealed hidden cities. Since the characters refused to lie down, that is now a ten-part series, holding back the publication of her trilogy of tales of space cowboys in the Viridian system.

When not writing and editing, Jemima loves to relax with her animals, watch birds and get out of the house as much as possible—not difficult when one lives in a beautiful part of the UK.

*****~~~~*****

Signals

by Erica Ruppert

Estella lay awake, searching her dark room with wide-open eyes for the source of the sound. She could see the night sky where the window shade had crept up, a slice of deep violet showing bright against the black of the room. But the sky was quiet, and the streets below as well. She could think of nothing else in the close darkness that would make any noise. But she could hear a barely audible note, almost a chime, that she could not place.

She had heard the sound in the background of the television's blare, a flickering ring that she thought was a bad signal. She turned the set off, and the sound persisted. Then she thought it might be a lightbulb starting to burn out, and dismissed it as an annoyance.

But now the lights were out, the apartment was silent, and the sound still intruded, intermittent, almost musical and low as a whisper. Each time Estella thought she had figured it out it stopped, only to resume after a few minutes.

She got up and stood in the middle of her small room. She listened, breath held, waiting for the sound to repeat. She heard the distant creak of the house's timbers settling in the cool night, heard the tick and ping of the radiators.

And there, so faint she could not tell if it was the thrum of her own blood inside her ears, a ringing like struck crystal that sang out and faded and sang out again.

She gasped, then caught her breath in again, afraid of drowning the sound out. But it escaped her.

Estella went to the window and pulled the shade all the way up. There was too much light pollution to see any stars, but she knew they were there. She flicked her fingernail against the windowpane, and listened to the dull plink on the glass. It was not the sound she wanted.

She crawled back into her bed, pulling the blankets up around her ears. The crinkle and scratch of her hair against the pillowcase kept her awake for a long while.

...

Waking was an effort. Estella wished she could call out sick, but it was easier to just push through the exhaustion.

She tuned in a dance music station for the commute, but she couldn't drown out the other music that floated just beneath it, sharp and full of dissonant quirks. She shut off the radio and listened to the traffic.

The office, when she dragged in, was a hive of distractions with voices rising and falling, the crisp shuffle of papers across cubicle-farmed desks, the click and tap of data input over and over again. She sat down quickly and logged in, trying to erase the unnamed song in her head. Under her fingers a clear cadence took shape. She struck the keys harder, typing nonsense across the fields. There was a lullaby comfort in the repetitious sound.

A phone rang, jarring across her rhythm. She blinked, and hit cancel on the mess she had typed in.

Claudia sat at the desk across from her, and came in a few minutes late, as always. She turned on her desktop and opened her music stream. A dated pop song drifted up from the computer's speakers, the sharp synthesizers piercing the otherwise white noise of the office. As the song built up to its jangling chorus, the strange high sound once again wormed its way into Estella's attention. It flowed along with the music, amplified by it but not in tune with it, distant, like a far-off bell.

Estella felt it tugging at her, the parasite sound a lure for something larger.

"Claudia, could you turn that off?" she said, too loudly. "I've got a headache today."

"Yeah, sure," Claudia answered with her normal cheer. "Why'd you even come in?"

Estella smiled, knowing how haggard she looked. "Exactly," she said.

...

Tommy had been the one who followed Alex Jones and *Coast To Coast AM* and anything he could dredge up about Area 51, the one who bought all the lizard men and alien conspiracy crap. His interest had grown from a quirk to a hobby to an obsession, and was a large part of why Estella had finally kicked him out.

Tommy had also talked about the music of the spheres, as if it were something he could tune in if he just kept still enough. It was twisted into his theories about alien overlords and human-alien breeding programs and cover-ups, to the point where Estella let it all wash over her without paying attention to his ramblings.

But after last night she couldn't stop thinking about some of the theories he had gone on about, about how certain resonances could change things, alter perceptions, twist the inner workings of a human mind.

Tommy had gone too far out, she reminded herself. Tommy was nuts.

The workday eventually ended, and Estella escaped the limits of the office. The sky already purple at five o'clock, and the wind carried a bite that hinted at snow. She sat in her car for a few minutes with the engine running, waiting for the heat to come. She watched other people get into their own cars and drive off to join the crush of rush hour traffic. She didn't realize she was drowsing, until a high, trembling note started her out of her trance.

She looked around the half-empty garage for the source of it, but it seemed to come from somewhere close to her. Inside the car. Inside her head. The note rose and fell like an intonation before it faded.

She shivered. She might have made sense of it, if it had gone on.

She turned on news radio and cranked up the heat, filling the car with chatter and moving air and pushing away the idea that she had inherited some of Tommy's crazy.

She didn't want to be nuts, too.

...

At home and safe inside her own walls, Estella searched out some of the sites Tommy had followed. None of them were on the first page of the searches, but she dug them out. What she uncovered was a cross-section of rabid dogma decked out in 1990s graphics, with yellow and red fonts splashed across black backgrounds and obviously shopped photos screaming for attention. Other sites were much more professional looking, but the prose was still riddled with paranoia.

She read them all, websites, blogs, subreddit threads. She followed links within pages. The message boards were the worst. The conviction disturbed her more than the content. She felt herself sinking slowly into the fearful mindset that generated such bleak conspiracies. But following their logic required a leap of faith she would not make.

It was nearly four in the morning before she closed her laptop. She didn't feel healthy after what she had read. Thin, spitting rain hit the window in a rapid tick-tick-tick. She tried not to find any pattern in it.

...

Estella called out of work the next day, claiming a migraine.

The house felt different during the day, like a bubble of empty space with her apartment floating on top. She slept on and off through the morning, restless, knowing what she was going to do, and knowing it was a mistake to do it.

She had deleted Tommy's number after they broke up. She scrolled through her contacts, trying to figure out which shared friend would be the least inquisitive. Finally, she called Maria.

"I don't think he has a phone anymore. I think it's turned off. I haven't tried to call him in a long time," Maria told her.

"All right," Estella said. "Do you know anyone else who would still be talking to him?"

Maria hummed as she thought. "Maybe Teddy," she said.

"Teddy?" Estella asked. "Do I know Teddy?"

"You've seen him. He hangs out at the One-Stop on Twentieth Street. Tall guy, skinny, with just a beard and no mustache."

The tune Maria had hummed worked its way into Estella's thinking. She could still hear it, high and soft, a distraction that teased at meaning. With it playing in the background of her attention, Estella could not remember anyone who looked like Maria's description. It didn't matter, though.

"That's right. I know him. So, do you have his number?"

Maria giggled. "Teddy's one guy who never has a phone."

"Okay," Estella said. "Thanks."

"Stell?" Maria said. "Are you okay?"

Estella stopped herself from sighing. "Fine," she said. "No problems."

Maria paused. "Call me some time," she said. "When you're not looking for Tommy."

"I will," Estella said, but Maria had already disconnected.

...

Teddy still hung out at the tiny neighborhood deli his cousin owned, using the rarely used rear dining room as an office of sorts. He. . . facilitated things, Estella recalled. She ducked through the wooden bead curtain that separated the dining room from the store, stirring a faint clatter that announced her.

She heard the steady tapping of fingers on wood before she entered the room. Teddy was at a corner table, rapping out a solid beat against its top as he leafed through a dog-eared notebook. She recognized him.

"Hey, Teddy, long time," Estella said. "I'm looking for Tommy."

"Do you see him here?" Teddy asked, never breaking his beat.

Estella unzipped her coat, already overwarm. "Maria said you might know where he is."

"Stella, lovely Stella. Haven't seen you around," Teddy said with greasy charm.

She shrugged. "Been working."

Teddy smiled.

"Haven't seen Tommy in about a year," he said.

Estella looked away from him. "All right," she said. "But if you do, tell him I need to talk to him."

"What for?" Teddy asked. "He wasn't any good to you."

"I know," she said. She paused, deciding how much she should tell him. How much she had to tell. Another beat, separate from Teddy's, caught her ear. She saw the metronome ticking away on the windowsill.

He followed her gaze.

"It helps," he said. "You should get one."

"Maybe," she said. "Look, Teddy, what Tommy used to go on about, the music of the stars and all that—"

"Spheres," Teddy said.

"Spheres. Right," she said. "I wanted to ask you, what do you think about it?"

Teddy cracked his knuckles and stretched his arms out in front of him. He resettled himself in his chair and resumed tapping.

"Have you ever heard of apophenia?" Teddy asked, and laughed when she shook her head. "That's what they call it when you can hear a song in some random sound that's repeated enough. Your mind makes music out of it."

"Is that what's happening?" she asked. "Is that what Tommy figured out?"

Teddy laughed again, but there was an edge to it. "Tommy didn't figure out anything."

He slapped his hand against the tabletop.

"Tommy thought he did, but he was wrong. He let the sounds in his head get to him, and then he disappeared. I don't think anyone has seen him since that happened. I think he's gone, Stella. Gone to wherever he thought the music would bring him."

"Where would that be?"

"Who knows? Could be downtown, could be Atlantis. You never know with him."

"You sound like you might believe him," she said.

Teddy stared at her for a long moment. "And you don't?"

Estella shook her head in quick denial. "Tommy lost it," she said. "There's nothing there to believe."

"Okay," he said. "If I see him I'll tell him to find you."

She smiled and nodded. She knew she had been dismissed.

...

The night had grown colder since she entered the deli, and she pulled her coat's collar up around her ears as she walked back to her car. The air smelled of ice. The sky above her rolled like ink spilled in water, darkness swallowing the yellow light of the city. She felt it peering down at her, watching to see what she did.

When she got back home she left a message on the voicemail at work. She wouldn't be in again tomorrow. She thought she was coming down with something. Then she pulled the shades against the bright night, buried herself in her blankets, and willed herself to sleep.

In the morning, she went across town to a music store and got a metronome. When she got back she emptied out the cartons of keepsakes that filled the coat closet to find her Nonna's old wristwatch. She wound it, and it ticked, relentless and unmusical. She put it on her wrist and wrapped her hand around it. It was like another pulse.

Teddy was right. It helped. The steady rhythm did not allow the other music any room to turn or grow.

The day stretched out around her. She wasn't sure what to do with herself. She revisited some of the conspiracy sites but in daylight they seemed silly and ugly and probably loaded with viruses. She stretched out on the sofa and tried to nap. It didn't work. She realized she was waiting for something.

By midafternoon a fine, dry snow had begun to fall, sifting down like sugar over the narrow lawns and closely parked cars. She watched the snow glitter against the greying sky until it was invisible outside the cones of the streetlights. Plows rumbled by.

She started when her phone rang, buzzing in her hand. She didn't recognize the number.

"Who is this?" she said as a greeting.

"Stella, it's Maria," came the voice. "Are you okay?"

"Yeah, I was sleeping. What's up?"

74

"It's Tommy," Maria said.

"Did you see him?" Estella said, too quickly. "Did you tell him to call me?"

"Stella—" Maria began, but then her voice was gone in the rush of a coming storm. The sound that came through rose and fell like wind, like a whistle, trilling and rustling and full of motion.

"Hello?" Estella said, loud and frightened.

"Hello," a voice warbled back, like birdsong. "Hello, Estella, hello."

It was not Maria's voice.

"Tommy?" she cried.

A high note trailed up beyond her hearing, any words it carried stretched past meaning. The note dropped again, resolving into a cadence like speech.

"Listen," it sang. "Listen. Listen. I'll tell you what I've seen."

A burst of static cut across the sound. The signal stuttered and dropped.

"Tommy?" Estella asked again, but the phone was dead.

She could still hear the storm-song, off-kilter and wild. It was in her head. It was in the sky.

After a while of listening to its whisper and taunt she put in her earbuds and logged into a streaming channel that played only ocean sounds. The crash of waves in her ears and the steady knock of the metronome on the table drove out the strange music and kept it at bay. She sat and watched the snow come down, afraid to sleep again.

...

In the dark of early morning Estella tugged the buds from her ears. The ocean was not enough, after all. The music had found a way to twist the metronome's steady, steady beat, changing it, altering the rhythm.

She still felt something curious waiting to get in. Waiting for a song to carry it across whatever void

75

separated it from her. Waiting for her to listen, to hear. She sighed, and her voice was a way in.

Inside her, behind her breastbone, a trickling chime rang out like breaking glass. She froze, frightened and excited and lost. How could it be so clear through all her flesh?

It rang again, in rhythm with the beat of her heart, with the pace of her quickened breath, with the throb and pulse of the stars shining sharply above her.

She sucked in and held her breath, to bring herself to the point of stillness, where she did not make ripples in the sound that cascaded around her. There, now. The stars, the moons, the travelers between, that Tommy had joined.

She could hear them, in the dark.

About the Author

Erica Ruppert has been published in, among others, *Turn to Ash, Unnerving, PodCastle,* and *Weirdbook.*

*****~~~~~*****

Night on the High Desert

by Connie Vigil Platt

There have always been strange lights to be seen in the midnight sky of the high desert. Maybe it is the altitude or the clear air. The old folks said it was St. Elmo's Fire. Usually that is phenomena seen on the ocean. The desert has been considered to be like the ocean by some people, so perhaps that is why the covered wagons were called Prairie Schooners.

The blazing hot sun beats down relentlessly on the milling cattle and riders in the desolate wasteland. Dust swirls around horses and on the men, blocking out the bright cobalt sky.

In 1890, October is the time for hard-working cowboys to ride long and hard to get the herd to market.

October is the time for ghosts and goblins to ride the night sky, if you are prone to believe in such things.

Tory Dawson had long ago outgrown ghost stories and things that go bump in the night: goblins were used to scare little children into being good or going to bed. What kind of twisted parenting is that?

October is also the time when certain planets are aligned with the earth. The time when it is easiest for space travel. This is the time of year when a portal may open wide enough to allow travel between these planets. Martians are well aware of this phenomenon and use it to their advantage.

Since it was time to round up cattle, it was the best time to amass specimens for scientific study. The Martians like to collect large animals such as cattle and horses for experiments. Naturally the best place to do this gathering is the western states, where there are there are huge herds of cattle and few people to observe a space ship landing.

If you should look at the night sky in the West, you might see that some stars appear to be closer together and nearer the earth than others. At times you might even see what seem to be two moons sailing in tandem across the otherwise clear sky.

After a hard day of work, Tory Dawson was too tired to look at the sky.

Jacob Pickens, the head foreman of the giant Diamond R cattle ranch, had sent Tory to pick up the payroll for the ranch hands. The herd was sold, the fall work was over, and it was time to pay off the men. Some would stay for the winter, but most would head for warmer climates.

The Diamond R was owned by a group of easterners who seldom visited the remote region. When they did come they usually brought their women with them. One of the owners had a daughter who came when she was not in some expensive boarding school. Dawson thought that was one attractive woman. A waist so small she could have used a hatband for a belt. Hair black as a moonless night, caressing her shoulders and reaching her tiny waist, emerald green eyes, watching him as he went about his duties. With cherry red lips that smiled at him every time he turned toward her, she was a cowboy's dream, one that he could see in the smoke of lonely campfires, a fantasy for the long winter nights in a remote line shack. It might be fun to see if that little back haired filly was as serious as she acted.

Tory had been a cowboy most of his life. When he was twelve or thereabout, he left home for greener pastures or for a better life than was to be found on his parents' poor dirt farm. All they had were debts and hopes for rain. The only thing they could give him was the ability to work hard and to appreciate having a paying job. Tory had worked himself up from horse wrangler to being straw boss or second foreman.

Tory could fork a bronc as good as any and better than most. His loop always hit the mark when he roped an animal. He could take care of himself in a barroom brawl or dance a reel with the prettiest girl. He was an all-round cowboy, and handsome enough to make the ladies' hearts flutter. Men wanted to be like him, and women wanted to be with him. He was a bit of a gambler, but then anybody who makes his living off the land is a gambler. It doesn't take bright lights to make a bet.

Tory went to the bank to deposit the money for the sale of the cattle and get cash to pay off the men. While he waited for the ranch's payroll to be prepared, he spent his time in the saloon, gambling and drinking. By the time the bank clerk came to tell him the payroll was ready he had won a Frazier saddle and a Stetson hat from cowboys from another ranch. He gave the losers his old saddle and hat to go home. Between the drinking and winning at cards, he was giddy, heady with joy. He had a good horse, a fine saddle, and a nearly new hat. He was riding an outstanding line-back buckskin horse he called Chico, which was Spanish for little one. Life was good.

Now it was to the ranch, away from town and bright lights, across some of the most desolate wasteland this side of purgatory. The local people called it the *Malapis* or "Bad Lands," partially because of the unusual twisted rock formations, and partly because it was considered to be a place where outlaws could hide from the law. Some honest citizens avoided it even in the daytime, but it was the shortest route back to the ranch. The hot, dry wind moaned its usual dirge, whipping small branches and tumbleweeds before the horse and rider, as if it was trying to stay ahead, and then twisting off in another direction. In the distance he could hear the roll of thunder and the flash of lighting stabbing holes in the dark clouds.

The red ball of the sun sank into the horizon as he left town. If Tory had looked up, he might have seen a star that was a little brighter, a little closer, and moving faster than the other stars in the sky. A star that could even be considered to be following him. It would never have occurred to him to consider a space ship.

Tory was used to being alone and rather liked it most of the time. Today, however, he was proud of himself and would have liked to have a friend to talk to and tell about his good fortune. He smiled to himself, thinking about the black-haired girl of his dreams. He could see her in wisps of fog or in the clouds of the setting sun. Still, he wished he had more company than his horse. He needed someone to talk to, not a dream. When he was ten miles out of town, he heard a soft clip-clop behind him, the echo of another horse on the rocks. A wave of terror washed over him as he remembered he had all the money for the other cowboys. He slowed his horse; the moon came out from behind a cloud, now shining almost bright as noon. The clip-clop behind him slowed also. The moon disappeared again, throwing shadows over the landscape. A twisted cedar tree became a hold-up man, a cactus turned into a growling coyote. Every rock was a disguise for an outlaw. Tory was not afraid, he told himself, but everyone knew when he left the saloon and that he was carrying quite a lot in his saddle bags. There were also the two unhappy cowboys that had played cards with him. Out of the corner of his eye he could see a shadow keeping pace with him. He kicked Chico into a trot; the rider behind him speeded up. He felt as if a hand closed around his throat. It was too far to the ranch; for all he knew there were more riders ahead. There was no way to outrun the shadow rider. The only thing to do was to face him right here. If there was a showdown, well, so be it. Tory had always been able to take care of himself. He was a good shot with his handgun and could take care of himself in a barroom brawl, so he was confident that he would be the winner in a fair fight. He turned his horse to confront the rider. There was no one in sight. He had vanished into the night. Out of the corner of his eye, Tory saw another rider. He was right—there was more than one.

"Who's there?" Tory called, "Show your face." No reverberation disturbed the night air.

Tory had heard of men finding cattle that had been killed and mutilated. Whoever did the act then left the carcass to rot. The blood appeared to be sucked out. Sometimes vital organs were missing, but there was never any sign of what killed them. No one had been able to find any indication who had done these terrible killings. There were never any tracks or sign of a human or known animal. Thinking about it made Tory edgy.

The wind blew cold, icy fingers lightly brushing his cheek. He heard only the howl of a lonesome coyote. Tory nervously sat on his horse, trying to look in all directions at once. He dropped his hand to his hip. His fingers caressed the butt of his Colt .44.40 single-action revolver. His horse trembled under him, side stepping and prancing, jittery, getting hard to hold still, sensing his master's excitement. Tory pulled severely on the reins, trying to calm the animal.

Beads of cold sweat popped out on his forehead. He reached up to brush them out of his eyes. Something touched his hand. An owl screeched in warning. He felt the faint swish of wings behind him. His head whipped around. He touched something lying against his cheek.

His fingers pulled the string away from the rim of his new hat, leaving him holding the edge of the brim in his hand. He held it up before his eyes, staring at the thread still attached to the material of the brim. As realization washed over him, he began to laugh, just a small chuckle at first. Then a real gut-busting laugh, "Imagine, of all people, me, Tory Dawson, spooked by a thread off his own hat. I should have looked it over better before I agreed to the bet." He spoke aloud, bathing in the sound of his own voice. Chico's ears twitched at the noise, laughter still floating in the night air. Tory drew his pistol and shot in the air to let off tension. The sound echoed against the rocks bouncing back at him.

"Come on Chico, let's go." He patted the neck of his line-back buckskin horse. He touched the horse lightly with his spurs. Together they moved forward.

He relaxed as he rode. By the time he had traveled several more miles he could make fun of himself. He had been a little too cocky, had a little too much to drink, and a little too much imagination. He sang trail songs to steady his nerves as he rode. It always calmed the herd, so it should calm him too, like a boy whistling in the graveyard. The night became dark, quiet. No glowing eyes, no evil flutter of bat wings.

About seven miles from the ranch sat an old abandoned school building that nobody used any more for anything but a landmark. When he first saw the outline of the bell tower it was apparent he had gone out of his way. He realized where he was now, even if he couldn't figure how he had got lost on the trail and gone the long way around. As he got closer, it looked like someone was having a party. There were lights dimly shimmering, faintly off white, the indistinct strains of music, shadows swaying in the windows.

"Hey Chico, this is what we need, we'll just stop a while, have a few dances with some pretty girls before we go on our way. I wonder who is having a party, though. I would have never believed that building was in good enough condition to have a party. Oh well, come on Chico, let's have a good time."

As he rode closer, clouds covered the moon; in the dimmer light the music seemed to get louder—piano, violins, guitars, banjos, and an instrument he couldn't recognize. A high voice sang lyrics in a language he couldn't understand. The tune carried on the breeze was not one familiar to him, and the beat seemed a little harsh for dancing. That didn't bother him, he would be able to pick up the tempo. Most horsemen had natural rhythm learned from long hours in the saddle.

Gentle laughter rippled through the air. He could see horses and buggies tied up in front. Although he didn't recognize any of them, he knew he would be welcome. The code of the West was to welcome everybody, even strangers. Invited or not, he would be accepted, no questions asked. It was rude to ask where you came from. He turned in the saddle to make sure the saddlebags were full of money and secure before he dismounted. When he turned back and faced the building again, the music was gone, no lights, no laughter. The horses and buggies were gone. All that was left was a tumbled-down building with vacant windows staring like empty eye sockets. He shook his head; the moon came back out, showing only the sagging roof and gaping open doorway of the abandoned building.

Tory turned his horse, visibly shaking. As he rode away, he heard music, the hint of girlish giggles. He looked back at the building and again saw the horses tied at the hitching rail, heard the dance music. Tory dug in his spurs and galloped away.

Behind him little humanoid creatures with a greenish glow surrounding them stumbled out of the doorway, holding long-necked bottles and chuckling foolishly at the prank they played on the cowboy.

"Come on," one called in a high-pitched voice, giggling girlishly, "If we don't leave now we'll miss our ride. We have all the samples we need for this trip."

"If we keep breathing this strange atmosphere, we'll be so inebriated we won't be able to get on the ship," one with a deeper voice agreed.

"I thought he was cute; I wanted to take him with us," pouted the third Martian as she climbed aboard the ship.

"We'll have some stories to tell around the break room when we get back this time," the leader said.

The sky burst with a flood of light as a saucer-shaped object floated across the horizon. Green glowing faces looked down out of the portholes, watching the cowboy ride away at a full gallop.

Tory, in a hurry to get back to the ranch, didn't turn around or look up at the sky, and he never saw the space ship as it glided across the night sky.

About the Author

Connie Vigil Platt, a fourth-generation cattle rancher, grew up on the high plains of southern Colorado. She has ridden with the fall roundup, branded with a hot iron, fed cattle horseback, and hauled supplies to line camps.

As an Old West history buff not content to see the old traditions disappear, she now devotes full time to Western writing. She has been published in Australia, Canada, England, and Japan as well as the United States.

*****~~~~~*****

Dispatches from the Eye of the Clown
by Justin Short

Tuesday, 8 July

Houston, we did it. We found a world where it rains clowns.

Thursday, 10 July

Yes, Houston, we're still here. Alive and well. Radio was giving us grief for a day or two. Please send my complaints to the manufacturer.

Per your request, I will confirm our last transmission. We found a world where it rains clowns. That's clowns with a C. *C-l-o-w-n-s*. Plural. I hope this removes all ambiguity.

However, in order to maintain the fullest degree of scientific accuracy, I will further clarify my statements. Yes, the rainfall literally arrives in the form of clowns.

But the clowns are not alive. They're not full-bodied.

When it rains, it rains their severed heads.

Their faces are painted in the garish fashion typical of clown subculture, with exaggerated streaks of white over the eyes and lips. They generally have red rubber

85

noses attached to their nostrils. Occasionally we encounter a face without the ridiculous prosthetic, but not often.

The hairstyle is always an afro wig. Normally it's rainbow-colored, but now and then we find one with a cotton candy dye job. The ratio of rainbow hair to cotton candy hair is nineteen to one. I don't know if this has any statistical relevance or not.

As you know, we lost most of our crew in the accident leaving the debris fields of Hermod Alpha. Only my wife and I remain. It has been a difficult adjustment, to say the least.

The sky is getting darker. I think a storm is coming.

Saturday, 12 July

Houston, we received your message. To be quite blunt, *how dare you.*

Deila and I are the ones stranded here. Not you. If your academics doubt our sanity, I submit the following. There are almost infinite worlds out there. The number is staggering. Billions of planets, untold parallel and perpendicular universes. I've personally led expeditions to planets where it rains glass. Diamonds. Sand. Sulphur.

Why not clowns?

Do you think we asked for this?

No. We asked for the resources to chart the Nord subsystem. We asked for appropriate safety precautions. We didn't ask for our companions to die horribly. We didn't ask to crash-land on a bizarre circus planet.

Not that you care, Houston, but Deila and I are getting along quite nicely. Our shelter is sturdy and safe. Somehow we manage to sleep through the night in spite of the constant *honk-honk-honk* of rubber noses hitting our roof.

We collect the rain in a series of bags near our makeshift latrine. We use these non-potable clown heads for laundry and bathing.

Taking a shower here is quite unsettling. Just lathering up will give you nightmares. But the worst part is the end, when you're toweling off and waiting for those grinning, dead faces to swirl down the drain.

Deila and I argue about what to call this world. We refuse to wait for acknowledgement or approval from Earth. The planet is ours, and we will name it. We will update you once we find something suitable.

We stocked up on drinking water at the waystation on Odin Beta. But that was weeks ago. I regret to say the supply is running dry. Tomorrow morning I will set out across the valley to search for a source of clean clowns.

Sunday, 13 July

I had quite the day.

I left after breakfast. The sky was green and cloudless. I didn't think I would need an umbrella. Nevertheless, I was less than a kilometer from our shelter when I got caught in a sudden clownpour.

Rain barreled down. I felt myself go under. My lungs filled with clowns, and I couldn't get a breath. I spat and wheezed. My vision went white. I treaded clowns for a few minutes. Drowning was inevitable, I thought.

But I found an opening. I pulled myself onto a high boulder with a curved overhang and waited out the storm. I must have coughed up two gallons of clowns!

The point is: I'm okay.

Not long after my scare, I found what I was looking for. It was less than two kilometers from our new home. I give credit to Deila's topographic background. She was able to give me a pretty good educated guess about the lay of the land. She did this without equipment, without software.

But back to the discovery.

I stood on a sandy beach and overlooked a sea of clowns. Uncountable millions, their skulls rolling and churning like the oceans of Earth. It was unlike anything I've ever seen. I wish my camera wasn't destroyed back on Hermod.

I took a large sample and headed back home. Deila and I have been tinkering around with an old shuttle filtration system, trying to adapt it to our new home. I'm eager to test it.

I only hope they're not *saltwater* clowns.

Monday, 21 July

We worked our butts off for a week straight, but we did it.

I dug a primitive aqueduct from the lake to our camp. Maybe I should say from the *ocean* to our camp. Truth is, we don't know how large the body is, but there's no sense arguing nomenclature. *Lake* sounds less oppressive. Friendlier.

It was backbreaking work, but I'm thankful the terraformer wasn't completely busted; otherwise the job would have taken weeks.

After a few late-night adjustments, our filtration system is a go. I'll give you a quick rundown. First, it purees the severed heads. Then it filters out the rubber noses and hair and eyeballs and teeth, and blends the rest into a dark soup. Once that passes through the purification chambers, the result is quite drinkable. Granted, it's not Colorado spring water, but it keeps the body going.

It was a tough week. We decided to reward ourselves. Last night we took a bottle of Chambourcin to Clown Lake and watched the green sunset. The tide was high, and the sun reflected off the thrashing, bubbling clown heads. It was gorgeous.

Then we took a peaceful walk back home, and it was off to bed.

We've been here almost two weeks, according to our paperwork. We have yet to spot another lifeform, human or otherwise. Not so much as a mosquito or tadpole.

Sometimes I lie awake at night wondering about the rain. Where did it all come from? How could this many billions of clowns become decapitated all at once, and how could an entire ecosystem be based upon their leftover heads? Why are they absorbed by the soil, and why don't they decompose instead?

The implications terrify me. I worry one day we'll stumble across a pit of headless corpses and a mad ringmaster with a rain machine.

I certainly hope not.

Monday, 28 July

It was chilly today. Woke up to a thin layer of clown-frost on the windows. The air felt thin and bitter. When I exhaled, I could see my breath turn into almost-transparent clown vapor before my eyes.

I wonder if winter is approaching.

Monday, 25 August

We've just come out of a three-day blizzard. Second storm this month. The cold season is definitely upon us.

Our cabin is buried in clown heads at the moment. I took a measurement last night, and it was nearly 100 centimeters deep.

Luckily, we have blankets and warm clothing, and enough supplies to last several weeks. I hope when the clown-snow clears, we'll be able to see some flora. A few blades of grass, maybe. A dandelion. Moss. Even a measly weed!

It's not right, being in a place this dead. I want to see life! Even if I don't understand it.

Wednesday, 15 October

It's warm again.

To celebrate, we had a picnic at Clown Lake. Brought our bathing suits and went for a nice swim. The experience isn't as pleasant as swimming back home. It's rather like slogging through a ball pit. And just when you're getting into a good backstroke, a dead clown nostril hits you in the armpit and jerks you back to reality.

It's a strange world, but it's our world. We're excited to raise our child here.

That's right. I never told you, Houston.

Deila is pregnant. We've known for a while now.

Think about it! He'll be famous! The first human born on Payaso-5!

Oh yeah. Forgot to mention that we named the place. Well, that's what we decided to call it. *Payaso* for obvious reasons, and *5* to honor our crew members who died back on Hermod.

We think it's appropriate. If you don't like it, you can—

Deila wouldn't let me finish that transmission. I'll let you read between the lines, Houston.

Thursday, 25 December

Merry Christmas, everyone.

Nothing much to report. We've been on vacation.

We've seen deserts and oceans, gorges and canyons. Beautiful works of art, Houston. The loveliest was a massive clownfall. I'd compare it to Angel Falls in Venezuela. The clown heads tumble from the clouded peak of a mountain and flow into a gorgeous, winding river. The clown-mist at the base of the falls takes your breath away. The hazy rainbows are incredible. I know we've been away from Earth a long time, but I can't imagine ever wanting to go back. We've got everything we need here.

Who cares if it's a dead planet? We have each other.

And soon we'll have three. Words can't describe how excited I am.

Saturday, 4 April

Deila is going into labor.

Monday, 6 April

I'm a dad, Houston, but I wish I wasn't. I feel like I'm cursed. Like this whole place is cursed.

Deila is healthy. Thank heavens for that! But the baby. . . oh, that disgusting *thing*!

She gave birth late last night. I coached her through the best I could. It wasn't pretty. Poor Deila. She was in so much pain.

Finally she was near the end. The baby was crowning.

When he did, I nearly lost my sanity. He crowned *afro-first*!

I was forced to get over my shock quickly. Cotton-candy afro or not, we still had a baby to deliver. After the wig were those horrible painted eyes, and then he wouldn't budge. I had to grab our homemade forceps and pull him the rest of the way. The rubber nose got caught, you know.

He's horrible. He's a bodiless clown. He belongs to this awful planet, not to Deila and me. It's a sick prank.

At first I thought he was stillborn. I *prayed* he was stillborn. But then he opened his eyes.

It's impossible, Houston. It defies nature; it's against everything normal and good.

Still, he belongs to us. We're calling him Andrew.

Wednesday, 8 April

Something is wrong.

This morning, while Deila was nursing, I took a stroll outside. I walked along the aqueduct and tried to find some peace. When I reached a place a few hundred meters out, I noticed the clown heads bottlenecking and spilling over the sides. Their eyes were open. Their mouths moved up and down. They screamed silently. Their eyebrows were furious; their rubber noses, expressionless.

I'm imagining things. The clowns are dead. They're part of this messed-up environment, that's all. They're not living beings.

I closed my eyes and counted to thirty. When I looked again, they were back to normal. Dead. Flowing along without interruption.

This place messes with your mind.

Friday, 10 April

Houston, get us out of here!

It's Andrew. I know it's Andrew. Something about his birth ignited this place.

It's raining again. A regular monsoon.

But this time, *the clowns are alive.*

I see their crooked smiles. Waves and waves of smiles. It's knee-deep out there.

They wash against our walls and smash into our windows. I hear the *tink-tink* as they hit our metallic roof.

Andrew is laughing. It's the innocent laugh of a baby, even though we hear it from the mouth of a disgusting clown.

They're chewing through the door. In a few minutes, they'll be inside. We're going to make a run for it. Deila's in no condition to run, but it's our only chance.

We debated leaving Andrew behind. But whatever he is, he's still our kid. He's coming with us.

There's a mountain range to the west. Maybe we can find shelter there, if we can make it through the rain first.

Send the cavalry, Houston, if we still have one.

This will be my last transmission. Tell our parents we—

About the Author

Justin Short's fiction has previously appeared in places like *The Arcanist, DarkFuse Magazine, Issues in Earth Science,* and *Dear Abby.* He can be found online at www.justin-short.com.

*****~~~~~*****

The Beast and the Orb of Earth Deux

by Wendy Nikel

Today is April 4, 2115, and you're listening to the podcast transmission of "The Search for the Truth," live from somewhere just outside the constellation Grus. If you are receiving this transmission, please take note.

You are our witnesses.

I found something. And I think it's important.

If you're a regular listener, you already know my story, but for anyone just tuning in, let me just give you a quick recap: We've been out here for ten years now, trawling the solar systems in our beat-up SRV-49, which—for those of you unfamiliar with shuttles—is basically the equivalent of a motor home with a rocket booster attached. We call it the Beast. It's not much to look at, and after a few months, it took on a funky fried-egg smell we haven't figured out how to get rid of, but Mick and I aren't picky.

We're part of a loose group of independent explorers who took seriously the events that occurred on Mars in 2050 and what happened on Kepler-438b in 2062. We believe there's a major government cover-up at play here, and we plan to prove it by providing the inhabitants of Earth with physical proof of extra-terrestrial life.

Technically, what we're doing isn't exactly legal, as most of these areas we're checking out are considered "restricted" by the Earth Space Authority (ESA)—that megalomaniacal amalgamation of national governments' branches that claims to be "protecting humanity's space travel" but is really just drunk on its own sense of authority. For those of you who don't travel in space much, these guys are basically the border patrol of the galaxy.

And today, after ten years of searching and dodging ESA ships and investigating your anonymous tips, we found something.

So here's how it happened.

Yesterday at approximately 17:30 Central Standard Earth Time, we received an anonymous tip that directed us to check out Gliese 832c, an extrasolar planet orbiting a red dwarf, known in our circles by the moniker, "Earth Deux," because of its similarities to our home planet. One of our listeners had noted some strange radio signals coming from around that area, and we thought it was worthwhile to check out. The planets in the habitable zone around Gliese 832 are restricted and are frequently patrolled by the ESA, which is nearly a sure sign that *something* is going on there that they don't want anyone to find out about.

We pulled ourselves out of FTL just outside the orbit of Earth Deux, and—sure enough—something had either happened here recently or was about to. A bunch of ships were swarming around one general area, so we slipped into stealth mode and descended through the planet's thick atmosphere in the opposite hemisphere. I marked on a map where the ships were focused, and settled down for a nap.

A few hours later the ships left, and Mick woke me up. We gathered our supplies and went to check it out.

It wasn't too hard to discover the spot where the ships had been focused. There were only so many places where the giant federal ships could land, and they left their telltale butterfly-shaped markings in the hard-packed desert sand where they'd gathered. We opted to skip the space suits for this one; Earth Deux smelled bad, but its air was breathable.

Mick hobbled out of the Beast on the crutches we'd fashioned for him after he busted his leg up in his last really bad crash landing, and I followed behind, breathing in the putrid, metallic scent of Earth Deux's desert soil. After weeks of travel, *any* air smelled better than the recycled air of the ship.

"They did some digging," Mick said, gesturing to a place where the ground was particularly torn up. "You think they buried something?"

"Only one way to find out." I sighed, knowing that I'd be the one spending the next hours digging into the rock-hard soil. Mick could've had a chip installed in his brain that would have sped up the reconstruction of bone in his leg, but he doesn't want any government tech in his head. That's how they make everyone so complacent.

Anyway, I pulled out the shovel and my heavy work gloves and spent the next hour or so digging, until I'd finally unearthed what had been buried there. Mick took pictures (available on our site's gallery) through the entire process as documentation. After it was uncovered, Mick and I just stood there (well, I stood there; he sat on a rock) staring at it.

"I don't get it," he said. "What is it?"

Hell if I knew.

It was a pulsing, golden orb about three feet around. It wasn't like anything I'd ever seen before, and though it could've been some sort of advanced technology the ESA had hidden here for some reason, there was something strange. . . something *alien* about it.

"Roll it up here. I want to check it out," Mick said. I made a big show of grunting and groaning, but the thing wasn't actually very heavy; it might've been hollow inside.

When I'd finally rolled it onto the surface beside Mick, he reached out and placed a bare hand on it.

"Don't touch it!" I warned him—too late.

He let out a string of expletives.

"What? What is it?" I pushed the thing away from him.

"I. . . I think it healed me."

For the first time since the crash, Mick wiggled his legs. But he didn't stop at that. He jumped to his feet and threw the crutches aside, where they kicked up a plume of gray Earth Deux dust.

"Ha, ha! It healed me! This thing. . this. . . whatever-it-is. It's some sort of miracle! I mean, it tingled for a bit—felt really weird. But look! I can walk! Holy—" He touched the sphere reverently and looked up at me with wide eyes. "We have to take this thing with us. This is the proof we've been looking for. You know the legends just as well as I do—space explorers finding strange healing rocks in deserted alien temples."

"None of those stories have ever been proven."

In case you're wondering, there's plenty of these stories floating around, if you know where to look. If you check out our previous broadcasts, we'll sometimes reference them. Unfortunately, every time the explorers have tried to find the same place again, they're unable to. They return to the exact coordinates to find the planet wiped, a wasteland, as if they imagined the whole thing. Space madness? Maybe. Conspiracy? That's our bet. Especially since access to those places generally becomes "restricted" soon after such incidents.

"Isn't that why we're out here?" Mick raised his eyebrows. "To prove those folks who stumbled across proof of intelligent extraterrestrial life weren't crazy? I mean, I can *walk*, man! What more proof do you need?"

"How do we know it's alien? That it's not advanced ESA tech?"

"You see the ESA stamp on it anywhere?"

He had a point. The ESA wasn't known for its subtlety. They stamped that bold, red ESA symbol on *everything* they claimed as theirs, from ships to space stations to satellites to antennas to jeeps to space suits to the dried space food they distributed. Besides, why would they make something like this? A healing orb? It just didn't seem likely. No, they seemed more interested in *hindering* scientific progress, with all their restrictions and checkpoints and laws about what can and can't be taken back to Earth from space.

"Okay, so we're assuming. . . what?" I asked. "That the ESA found this alien tech somewhere and brought it here to bury it?"

Mick shrugged, testing out his now-working legs by kicking around clumps of rock. "Or, maybe the aliens were here first and buried the orbs themselves. The ESA showed up and chased them away but didn't realize they'd dropped something here?"

It was a possibility, but either way, something was off. The ESA might not be comprised of the brightest stars in the sky, but they ought to have seen the same evidence of the soil being disturbed that we did. It didn't make sense that they'd bury it, either, considering they had all those locked and guarded warehouses on Mars that they could store stuff in way more securely.

"So what do we do now?" I asked Mick, who was now trying to do the moonwalk.

"We document our find, package it up, and take it back to Earth as proof, of course. Finally, proof not only of intelligent alien life, but of a major ESA cover-up as well. We did it, man!" He offered me a high-five, which I reluctantly returned.

Even now, back on the ship with the orb tucked away safely in our cargo area and our route set for Earth, something doesn't feel right.

As always, listeners: If you are receiving this transmission, please take note. You are our witnesses.

...

Today is April 5, 2115, and you're listening to the podcast transmission of "The Search for the Truth," live from somewhere between the constellation Grus and the Milky Way galaxy.

The ESA is after us.

I'm not sure if they tracked us through our podcast or what, but they're on our tail, and Mick is flying the Beast like some kind of madman, flicking from FTL to slower-than-light at nauseating intervals in an attempt to shake them.

Hold on. Here comes another jump. Ugh.

Anyway, they caught up to us ten or fifteen minutes ago and sent us a signal to stop and allow them to board. Right. Like that's going to happen.

Mick sent me back here to document what's going on in case something happens to us. And probably just so I'd stop being a back-seat driver. We're putting on speed again. I don't know what's going to happen if they do catch up to us, but I doubt we'll be able to convince them that the orb's just a gold-plated exercise ball.

Oh, no. Something's wrong. The ship's stopped. Something's very wrong. Oh, don't fail us now, Beast.

Uh-oh.

In case you didn't hear that, that was the sound of our engine dying. We're stuck. No, we're worse than stuck. We're trapped. I expect the ESA to take all of thirty seconds to dock and break into our airlock, unless Mick can get the engine started again. I'm going to throw a bunch of junk on top of the artifact and hope they don't notice it. Regardless of what happens, I'm going to keep the tape rolling. Remember, listeners: you are our witnesses to whatever happens here. . . whatever goes down. They can't hide the truth forever. Not with all of you out there who now know what's really going on.

They're in the airlock now. The glass is frosted, but it looks like there must be two, maybe three, of them.

They're hacking into the lock. There's nothing else we can do now.

The door. . . it's opening. There—

Oh my—

We were wrong! We were wrong about all of it! They just took their helmets off, and—

No, lct go!

The ESA isn't *covering up* alien life! The ESA *is*—

[42 minutes of static follow]

About the Author

Wendy Nikel is a speculative fiction author with a degree in elementary education, a fondness for road trips, and a terrible habit of forgetting where she's left her cup of tea. Her short fiction has been published by *Fantastic Stories of the Imagination, Daily Science Fiction, Nature: Futures,* and elsewhere. Her time travel novella, *The Continuum*, was published by World Weaver Press in January 2018, with a sequel forthcoming in July. For more info, visit wendynikel.com

*****〜〜〜*****

Growing Smaller

by Jimmy Huff

In the amber of another sticky summer evening in Sacred Little, the faint voice of autumn spoke up like a sweet executrix. Change was in the air. The sidewalks were still. The city pool was deserted. But the local yokels rallied against the all-too-appealing prospect of air conditioning and reclining chairs; every able-bodied adult, and all the children, gathered at the fairgrounds instead. The carnival was in town.

Kilter could remember his first carnival, the great big roller coasters that climbed up into the sky. Running around with childhood friends and eating funnel cake until they were sick remained ingrained in his mind after all these years. Now approaching 40, Kilter considered it often—the child inside of him, carefully partitioned off by time. He hoped to hold onto that, and to share that part of himself with his eleven-year-old son.

"But where are the roller coasters?" Kilter muttered to himself.

"Hey, Dad," Dudley said, breaking Kilter's trance. "What's that?" The boy pointed at the giant tent with a banner which read *The Cabinet of Curiosities.*

"That's the sideshow," Kilter told him. "The freaks."

"*Freaks*," the boy echoed. "What's that mean?"

"It means—'different.'"

"Can we go inside?" Dudley asked.

"Maybe later," Kilter told him. "But it's not really for children."

"Why? Is it scary?"

Considering the question, Kilter said, "It can be." Though, admittedly, he'd snuck into the freak tent all those years ago when he was Dudley's age. It wasn't so bad. One man breathed fire. A woman had been sawed in half. Another woman had a beard. There was a six-legged dog, but mostly it lay in the corner nipping at fleas. The only genuinely disturbing aspect had been the baby genius, who couldn't have been older than three years of age but spoke more eloquently and well-informed than anyone Kilter had ever met or probably ever would. It was eerie. "Your mother would object," he decided—although that was nearly reason enough to let the boy have his way. "Maybe when you're older."

"She never—" Dudley began. But he let it go there. He wasn't one to pout, and in that regard and so many others which made Kilter's heart swell, Dudley was mature for his age. The boy looked away momentarily. And a smile formed on his face.

"Say, Clem!" a voice boomed. A hairy man in a disproportionately small speedo sat perched above a drum of water. "Sink the fink!" he shouted at them. "First throw's a dollar!" Out to the side was a target on a pendulum; it moved side to side at alternating speeds. Presently the carney threw a ping pong ball at Dudley. He had a bucket of them, and there were ping pong balls everywhere.

Dudley giggled and pointed. "Sink him, Dad!"

"Yeah, Dad," echoed the crusty carney. "If you *can*!"

"All right," Kilter said. He paid the carney overseeing the game and received his ammunition.

Presently he stepped into the spray-painted circle on the grass, stretched his arms and legs, and readied himself.

And a ping pong ball hit him upside the head. Dudley laughed. Kilter turned, indignant, readied himself once more, and threw the ball—with contact. But nothing happened.

"Whoa," the carney cackled. "Close! But we're not playing horseshoes!" He laughed and threw a ping pong ball at them.

"Try again, Dad!" Dudley shouted. "Sink him!"

"Okay, okay," Kilter said. He stretched once more and handed over another dollar.

"*Two* dollars," said the carney. He was tall and bird-faced, just as unpleasant as his partner.

"*Two dollars*?" Kilter said.

"The price doubles every time, sir," the carney informed him. "But if you wish I can slow the speed of the target." He did so, now, marginally.

"Let's go," Kilter said. "It's rigged."

"*Rigged*?" the carney said peevishly. He picked up a ball, took a step forward, and threw. Bullseye. He had an arm like a cannon; this was his life's work. The platform gave way and the fink dropped into the water like a rock.

Or did he trip it, himself? Kilter wondered. This was a classic alibi store: there was only the illusion—albeit palpable—that the game could be won.

Kilter laughed to himself and ruffled Dudley's hair. "We'd better get moving if we're going to see it all." This game would soon be impossible, if it wasn't already. A gentle wind picked up as night settled in.

Dudley nodded and giggled. "Let's ride *that*!" he shouted, pointing and leading the way toward a giant flat screen TV.

"I don't think that's a ride, son," Kilter said. In colorful lettering, the screen said *Tilt-a-Whirl.* Then the picture ebbed away, and a video began playing. People mutely laughing, spinning, twirling and whirling round

105

and round on a gorgeous thrill ride. But where was it? Kilter looked around. Behind the TV were row after row of folding chairs, people sitting here and there wearing strange helmets. "What is this?" he heard himself saying.

"Wave of the future," said a nearby carney. "Every bit of the excitement, none of the danger or hassle." He grinned knowingly with missing teeth, and said, "Just a dollar."

Dudley stared into the TV, enchanted. Kilter paid the man, and presently they were seated.

There was no "*You Must Be This Tall to Ride*" sign. No cacophonous clicking and raging metal objects which could kill as quickly as delight. Was it that fine line which made these rides so appealing? Kilter wondered, feeling a little bummed, a little held over. We're being "gypped," he thought, as they used to say when the world wasn't so anal. Dudley sat on the edge of his seat, giddy and watching the family beside them in the chairs grinning madly, laughing and shouting. They leaned this way and that; they threw their hands up in the air at times. "Ooh," they said. "Ahh!"

The carney returned and handed them helmets. Dudley snatched his away and strapped it on. "Whoa!" Dudley shrieked almost at once, giggling wildly.

Kilter regarded the strange helmet, still unsure what to make of it. Like an astronaut's globe, but smaller, and without the open face panel. A timer said, *3:46*, then *3:45, 3:44.*

"Strange time to be alive, ain't it?" said the carney. "Put it on. It's not so bad."

Kilter slid the helmet onto his head—

And there he was, again, all those years ago, a child let to play. And the world, these fairgrounds, a playground. Kilter stood and looked around. How entire it was—the projection. The *sounds*. The smell, even—was that funnel cake? Or was it just the well-worn helmet? His virtual reality began to spin.

106

"Sir," said the carney. "Please remain seated during the ride."

...

Electric light shone down on the fairgrounds. Kilter sipped a beer and padded around aimlessly while Dudley and some friends rode the various virtual rides. The wind picked up a little.

"Things sure change, don't they?" a voice said.

"You've got that right," Kilter said, regarding the man. He recognized him from somewhere.

"Aaron York," the man said. "We went to school together."

That's right, Kilter thought. Aaron—*Aaron York.* "It's been a long time."

"Decades," Aaron said. "What line of work are you in?" he asked.

"I'm a climate engineer," Kilter told him.

Aaron stared blankly and said, "Oh."

"I work for ETC," Kilter said. "It's mostly research based work in regard to a sustainable future."

Aaron smiled. "Still fighting the good fight," he said.

Kilter didn't know what to make of that, but it was a kind thing for Aaron to say. He took a drink of his beer and pondered.

"Doesn't it bother you, though?" Aaron asked. "What they're saying about the world ending. Kinda makes the future seem like the wrong line of work to be in."

Kilter hadn't thought of it that way. And maybe he was right. Where had planning for the future gotten him? "What are you doing these days?" he asked, changing the subject.

"Oh, a little of this, a little of that," Aaron said. "I run a landscaping business, mowing lawns mostly. I tell ya, I'm ready for some cooler weather."

"It's on its way," Kilter said, taking a drink of his beer. He looked around at the hustling bustle of people passing from booth to booth, virtual ride to virtual ride, all wide-eyed and under the impression that anything could happen. It was in the air. Kilter took a deep breath, took it all in. Presently Dudley came bounding up.

"Could I borrow five dollars?" he asked breathlessly.

"Sure," Kilter said. And he smiled, handed him some money. Dudley grinned and ran off again.

"Good looking young man," Aaron said. "Where's his mother?"

"Where, indeed," Kilter said, withdrawn. "Probably counting all of my money, bill by bill." He finished his beer and crushed it. "We finalized our divorce today."

"Ah, well, I'm sorry to bring it up," Aaron said. "It may not seem like it now, but life goes on. On and on." He extended his hand. "I'm glad we ran into each other," he said.

"Me, too," Kilter said, accepting the handshake. "Take care of yourself." He tossed the beer can in a nearby trash receptacle and watched Aaron depart.

Kilter found himself seeking out the old-fashioned carnival attractions of his childhood. He was disappointed by how few there were. Presently he padded over to the *The Cabinet of Curiosities* and let himself inside. He walked into the heart of the melting pot, his head on a pivot, childlike. And then he saw him, the baby genius, alive and well after all these years.

The baby genius wasn't a baby anymore, but it was certainly him. He had the same plum-shaped nose and matted brown hair. He might've been one of the sharpest minds on the planet for all Kilter knew, and using his talents as a carnival sideshow of all things—still. Presently he spoke of the recently discovered supermassive black hole the world's experts were calling "Mother."

"Einstein was onto something," the prodigy said. His eyes were mercurial, meeting every gaze. "As Mother continues to sip up the Milky Way, our gravity will become increasingly affected. I expect time, too, will be altered." He didn't claim to be a fortune teller, but the small crowd regarded him as such. "As you know, Pluto has already begun to spiral out to space. They're right," he said. He didn't specify who *they* were, but it made Kilter uncomfortable. "Earth won't be lost in our lifetime; we're lost already."

Kilter considered this, his own thesis, as it were, written and then written again countless ways over the years. And there it was, unadorned and put so simply: *We're* the problem—whatever the problem may be. Mother's anger might even be disappointment, but that hardly made the situation more fortunate. He looked away from the prodigy and those prodding eyes, tore himself from the crowd, and padded on.

The sword swallower cut himself shaving. That's entertainment, Kilter thought.

He sheathed kodachis in his mouth, sweat beading down his cheeks and dampening the tiny, blood spotted squares of tissue stuck to his neck. Kilter could only look for a moment. Too much could go wrong in this act. He kept on walking.

Two displays caught his eye.

One was Bonnie and Clyde's getaway car, a 1934 Ford V8—an antique. A carney stood beside it shouting, "Genuine, genuine!" A hundred years later, nobody knew who Bonnie and Clyde were. Kilter, unsure, asked a man gawking, "Who were they?"

"They invented life insurance," the man said.

"Um," Kilter said. And he walked away.

The other display was Donald Trump's hairpiece, now given the pet name Rufus. There was still much speculation as to what happened to him after his presidency. Once his term had expired, he disappeared, never to be seen again. Rumor was Rufus ate him.

Kilter padded on. He approached a quiet crowd surrounding the sideshow's contortionist, a thin and nimble wisp wearing a black-and-white full-body spandex suit with crisscrossing lines. The design gave a constant illusion of changing size. Man or woman, it didn't matter—and probably that was the point. It was a curious performance. Perched on a small plateau at the center of a backlit stage, the contortionist sat curled up in a ball, a ball which seemed to shrink, near but never quite blinking out of existence. The degree of difference between the nothingness and somethingness was particularly moving. Presently the space behind the stage grew colorful, and on the wall words formed: *Summertime Sadness and the Self-instilled Inability to Grow.*

The contortionist rocked back and forth in a pulsating ball.

This continued for some time.

Then the writing on the wall faded away, and new words replaced them.

Remembering to Forget, Learning to Remember.

The contortionist sprouted from the ball, arms raised and spread in a V. And the growth continued until the figure was standing, arms still reaching as if pulled apart. Invisible strings held them there.

The crowd groaned.

On the wall behind the stage words said, *Food for Thought When Determinism Goes Hungry.*

The contortionist struggled visibly against the puppet strings, though to no avail. In fact, it made matters worse. Presently the figure was jilted down from its perch; arms out, the contortionist was led around the stage as if against his will. Stopping at a table, the hands lifted up a hammer and smashed a birdhouse to bits for no apparent reason. Then the figure was led to an easel where they painted a mustache onto the Mona Lisa.

The contortionist stopped, turned, and faced the crowd, arms hanging there. With great effort, the contortionist tore their arms free.

The crowd let out a sigh.

Kilter felt his arm twitch. He rubbed it and watched the contortionist climb back up on his perch.

Behind the stage, words said, *The Advent of Technology and Our Countless Failures to Imagination.*

The contortionist pulled one leg up and tucked it behind their head. They grabbed hold of their other leg, now, moved it forward and back in a strange manner. Finally, they tucked the other leg back as well. Then the figure rose up on their hands and scooted around absurdly.

Some of the crowd lost interest and wandered on. Kilter looked at his watch and decided he'd see one more bit. It was interesting.

The contortionist sat back in the center of their perch and fell into fetal position—and seemingly kept falling. The writing on the wall said, *Inner Child Let to Play.*

The contortionist lay there falling, legs moving ever nearer to their chest and ever away. Hands rose and fell in the form of birds. There might have been four hands—six, even. There were dozens of different birds. And there was an unmistakable fluttering sound. And a gentle breeze.

The hair on Kilter's neck stood up. He felt a little lightheaded. His bones buckled, but it wasn't the typical feeling of old age. It was something else. He felt more— nimble, more energetic. He felt smaller. He looked around and—

All around him a crowd of giddy, giggly children. And he felt young, too, like anything was possible.

Kilter made his way to the door. He ran, actually, and laughed. It was *fun*.

He momentarily met eyes with the baby genius as he passed him. The young man had regressed back to the child oddity Kilter remembered so vividly.

"The meek will inherit the earth," the baby genius said proudly. And he winked at Kilter.

Kilter smiled, parted the fabric door, and stepped back out into the fairgrounds.

Children, all of them; old friends and new. And presently Dudley came bounding over.

"I've been looking for you," Dudley said. "I have, I promise."

"That's okay," Kilter said. And he ruffled Dudley's hair playfully. "I must have lost track of time."

Dudley giggled. "I had fun," he said.

"You're not ready to *leave*, are you?" Kilter asked.

"Aren't you?" Dudley said.

"Heck no," Kilter said, laughing. "The night is young, my boy. And so are we." He nudged Dudley on the shoulder and grinned.

Dudley laughed. "You seem *different*."

The sound of string music drowned out the cacophony of the carnival. A cool, gentle breeze blew.

Other children wandered over, three girls and two boys. "Hey," they said simultaneously. "Want to ride *that*?" they said, pointing at a giant metal roller coaster called Apollo's Chariot.

Kilter stared in disbelief. It was exactly as he remembered it—Godlike, which was the idea. It was so big, and they so small. It was humbling, but it was more than that. It was *healing*.

Through the soupy string music of Apollo's healing lyre, Kilter felt a deep, abiding joy he had forgotten. "Heck yeah!" he shouted. And he heard himself giggle.

"Yeah!" Dudley shouted.

The children laughed and ran toward the roller coaster.

The seating on Apollo's Chariot was such that they sat in pairs. Dudley sat next to the boy named Blake. Blake had lightning-yellow spiked blond hair and no sense of his own volume. He shouted and jeered and was a lot of fun to be around. Kilter sat beside a girl named Gail, Blake's mother. But she looked far too young to be. And far too beautiful. Presently Gail struggled with her buckle. Kilter helped her.

"Here," he said, gently grabbing hold of the belt. And he regarded his hands, how small they were. And he felt small, vulnerable. He buckled Gail's belt.

"Thank you," she said sweetly.

Under a sea of stars Gail smiled at him, a smile as vast as the ocean above. Kilter hadn't kissed anyone since he was much older, and in a failing marriage, no less. He considered kissing Gail now. But there was all the time in the world for that. The roller coaster lunged into motion.

About the Author

Jimmy Huff is pursuing an MFA at Lindenwood University. His work has also appeared in *Dirty Chai, Eastern Iowa Review, Paddle Shots: A River Pretty Anthology, Vol. 2,* and other lovely places.

*****~~~~~*****

Titanrise

by Adrik Kemp

Dragging a moon through space isn't all it's cracked up to be. The accommodation is cramped and crowded, the company is woeful and the rewards negligible at best. I'm a designated T5. I could be a T4 on my better days, but I'd rather be a big fish. I'm not sure how they came up with the numbers in the first place, but it means we're four points behind the heavyweight T1s, who can probably just pull the moon themselves, and it also means we get bunked together, do longer, harder shifts, and get paid less. Glamour, it isn't.

I have the displeasure of sharing with Tania and Melody. Each room has four bunks, so it's a luxury that we have a spare bunk, apparently. I woke up a little before the others, so I've had time to think about what the hell I'm doing with my life while we're strapped to our beds on our backs. The riveted steel ceiling almost grazes my nose. The fluorescent light has tinged everything a sick yellow green. Tania is below me, and Melody is asleep on the other side, emptiness below her, floating because she likes her straps loose. Her hair is out and starting to billow around her face. Looks itchy.

Tania taps on the underside of my bunk, but I ignore her. She taps again. "Indi? You awake?" she says, knowing I am and that I'm deliberately not answering.

115

I grunt. I don't want to talk.

"You ready for today?"

No.

"You know, it's weird but I feel like I'm a bit stronger than before. Remember before you became a T when we thought you could just go up the levels until you reached T1? I know it's stupid, but the more we do this, the stronger I feel, and I know it's just an urban legend, but I'd love to be a T1 one day."

Wouldn't we all. T1s get their own rooms. They get their own bathrooms. I mean, what's not to want. But T1s, and T2s and T3s and so on in fact, are born, not bred, and the best we can hope for is to be on the higher end of our rating. And honestly, there's not much difference in terms of living conditions, and you have to lift more the further up you go, so I don't see the point in trying too hard.

"You know what else I want?"

Tania's not going to stop. I sigh, unclip my harness, and drift off the bed. "I'm going for a glide," I say, spinning the door lock and getting out before Tania can unbuckle and offer to come along with me.

The corridor is not quiet. T10s and T11s are dotted on the corners, making sure our ancient ship stays together and airtight. Their inane chatter fills my ears as I drift by them. I'm aiming for the greenhouse, but I've got to get through a lot of twisted access shafts before that, and the din is deafening.

Up through the centre of the ship, there's a repurposed elevator shaft. The elevator sits defunct at the base, and crew shoot up and down. The space is quieter here, given most engineering crew are standard and more stressed about everything, so I can relax somewhat. Up four levels, I take a sharp right, a long, windowless and unmanned corridor, until I reach the sealed, guarded greenhouse doors. Two T3s stand outside. A bit of overkill if you ask me. Brandy and Michele took the job

116

out of curiosity and boredom. They used to work in Hollywood, and did a couple of high profile security jobs before making enough money not to bother anymore. Brandy's parents were part of the Mars terraform too, so she's old money, but you'd never know it considering she went into security and adult entertainment.

"Hey," I say.

"Hi Indi, you wanna go inside?" Michele smiles. She's blonde, perfectly clean and crisp, an American dream circa 2003. A total throwback fetishist in other words. She's a typical shut-in, only taking jobs to get enough money to buy more boutique vintage 00s clothing.

Brandy's head is shaved, and she's got silver tattoos on her neck that glow brighter the more energy she's exerting. She loves an ero-high, and so do all her fans. Also helps that she shoots some of her footage in space. She smiles and runs her eyes down me, pulsing her tattoos while she does. She knows this makes people uncomfortable, but it's part of why I like her so much.

"Is Pete awake?" I ask.

Michele shrugs. "Stuffed if I know. Our job is to guard, not babysit." She unlocks the door. "But go see for yourself."

As the cold steel opens, verdant green growth all but spills into my vision. Vines tumble over trees and closed tanks of water teeming with small fish. Ferns and succulents dot every surface, and only the slightest path is visible within. I nod at Brandy, shooting her a wink, thank Michele and slide through. The air is thick, moist and hot. I shoot through the undergrowth until I reach Pete's alcove. He's awake, barely, floating in a cocoon of vines and flowers. I put my fingers in his yellow hair and rub his scalp. He turns and smiles at me, like a reflection of a human in an algae laden pond. Pete and the other greenhouse attendants are chlorokinetics. Pete is a C2, which means something to do with species differentiation and manipulation, but I'm honestly not even sure how they measure Ts, so Cs are out of my league. At any rate, he's a bit green around the edges. In fact, he sort of glows, especially when he's surrounded by plants, as he often is.

"Let me guess," he says, "Tania won't shut up?"

"I don't know how Melody sleeps through it. She's incessant. She was talking about being a T1 again. I mean, for God's sake, it's not going to happen, right. It's a stupid kids propaganda story meant to encourage us to serve the UN. She's so annoying."

Pete chuckles. It'd be annoying as well if he wasn't so cute. All zero-grav Cs are a bit smaller than your average human. A lot of people think Cs grow leaves and survive on nothing but sunlight and water, but those people are ignorant. They eat the same as everybody else. But sometimes Pete's hair does sprout little leaves. And he told me once that he grows little red flowers in spring, but I'm holding off on believing that until I see it.

"I'm just so done with it. Next job I take, better get my own room."

Pete smiles, his brown eyes crinkling. "You can always stay here. I'd like the company." He's in the middle of unfurling from his vine wrap.

"I'm sure they'd love that."

The last ivy trails into the air, and Pete floats up to me. He hugs me, and I breathe in the fresh scent of his hair. His body is warm and comforting.

"How long to Earth?" he asks.

"Not long, we should be able to see it from here. It's sort of why I came around."

Pete grins. "And here I thought you wanted to see me."

I can't help but blush. "That too. . . ."

Pete takes my hand and pushes up through the undergrowth. We fly through ferns and past tunnel-tanks brimming with fish. I brush my fingers against soft leaves, before we break through the small canopy to see the triple-layered glass and plastic dome that forms this vital section of our clunker of a ship. The greater ship is shaped like a fan, with the greenhouse dome at the middle of the centre vane. The inner six vanes are dotted with T cells, where my peers sit dragging our payload behind us. The outer two house the E cells, equipped with power generators in case the electrokinetics run out of juice and our force field goes down. There's always blue and yellow crackling lightning around the edge of our ship, but it's concentrated on the outer two borders. The Es tend to keep to themselves, and they're confined to their areas for safety reasons anyway. Not the most stable kinetics, if you know what I mean.

The body of our ship is uninhabited, since we're doing a drag to Earth and not a local terraform. They stopped doing them a few decades ago since realising the cost of transport and resources was unsustainable. It was destined to fail when the only people who could afford to become pioneers were rich and were never going to want to leave the good things they had going on Earth. And science fiction and history may have liked sending prisoners out to populate new worlds, but in the present, it's not really kosher to reward prisoners with free new lives on brand new, very expensive worlds.

I mean, eventually more people will move to Mars and Enceladus, but they're pretty sparsely populated right now.

On a terraform mission, the middle section houses GAPA teams. Geos and pyros work any volcanic activity and settle the continents. And aquas and aeros figure out the seas and skies. It worked pretty well, but like I said, we're a drag ship now, so no GAPA team required. Now they spend most of their time in orbit around Earth making sure our home planet is stable under the stress of its ever-multiplying new satellites.

Pete points a green fingernail and hairless arm out into space. It's a ways away yet, but the blue and green world of Earth is about the size of a tennis ball. The moon glows in orbit around it. Europa is a little further away than the moon but on a parallel orbit. And we can't see it, but Ganymede is on the other side of the planet, making its tripled orbit again.

"Home sweet home," Pete curls his arm around my waist and rests his head on my shoulder. His hair brushes my skin. It's cool to the touch, like foliage. I pull up and kiss him, closing my eyes against the greenhouse, the vision of Earth and its moons, and the ship that never sleeps all around us.

We stay locked together for a time, kissing and spinning above the trees while Earth and her satellites swell in space. I don't disentangle until the lights on the ship flip from white to yellow and we start the slowdown into Earth's furthest orbit.

One by one, the T vanes start clicking over to green as my fellow workers take their places for the final pull and stabilize. My spot is at the end of the third vane from the starboard side, and my light is decidedly not green.

"You better hurry." Pete kisses me again, and I all but melt against him. "I'll be here waiting when you're done."

I take a deep breath, most definitely not sated and now also pretty agitated, and float back into the trees, past the orchids and running water and out the door.

"Finished with him then?" Brandy's voice startles me. "Maybe I'll have a go next."

"Shut up," I say.

Feigning shock, Brandy cocks her head. "That's no way to talk to a T3, is it? Better apologise."

I take a deep breath. It's a joke, but there are protocols and you never know when a person's going to snap from lighthearted to dead serious. "Sorry, Brandy. Won't happen again."

Brandy leans over and smells my face. "Better not," she winks. "Next time, let me join you. Cs make me a lot of money on my channel you know."

I pull back. "Pete's not for sale."

Brandy shrugs. "Eventually you'll wanna settle down, and it'll take more than one drag to pay for that."

"I'll figure it out," I say, gliding off with more rage than I thought I had about my future. The warning lights slip from orange to red, and my heart races. I start pulling the handles on the walls and shooting through almost-deserted corridors down the bowels of the ship and into my vane. I swing past Melody, yawning and rolling her eyes at me. Tania glares at me too, but is focused on the payload. I slip into my seat and buckle up. The glass in front of me is tinted for now. I take a deep breath and close my eyes, waiting for the countdown.

The computer's voice is guttural in all our ears.

"Five. . .

"Four. . .

"Three. . .

"Two. . .

I exhale and open my eyes to look out the now-transparent window.

"One."

Earth's newest moon is vast before me. Clouds of putrid yellow cover glimpses of deep green and blue. Not trees or ocean, I know that much. The entire globe crackles with lightning, care of our E comrades. It's in our force field now, to avoid losing too much atmosphere on the long trip from Saturn. We took the liberty of bombarding the surface with fragments of Saturn's ice ring before encapsulating it, so there's a bit of activity on the surface while the tiny planetoid tries to deal with that. It's in an E field within the larger one as well, to avoid any inadvertent damage to us.

I concentrate on my quadrants, now superimposed over its surface on the window. Mine are behind, so it's a

121

strange overlay, as if the solid object is invisible, but I grab it with my superior mind's eye and balance it in myself.

"Brace," the ship's computer is in our ears. "Orbital target in three, two, orbital target reached. Brake. Pull. Brake. Pull." I'm sweating. I'm tired and hungry and my mind is drifting to Pete and his canopy, but I'm still listening to the interminable computer, still pulling and bracing and nudging the great big thing into place. The sun will contribute a lot to terraforming this one. The local GAPA crews will still have a lot to do, but not as much as when it was in orbit around Saturn. The ice crew is about a week behind us, so they'll have that to use as well. And any excess will likely go to Mars. Below, the slowing behemoth roils with power. Its new position in the solar system is already wringing changes on its ancient surface and in its core. "Brace. Brace. Hold." The computer stops. I'm straining along with all the other Ts to keep inertia from pushing the moon further along and into Earth. It's dangerous, but there's always a couple of T1s on standby around Earth for this or any other eventuality. And GAPA teams that can blow it up before it hits the planet if the T1s fail.

"Hold."

I sigh through gritted teeth.

"Hold."

"Optimal orbit reached. Stabilizing."

"Hold."

"Orbit stabilized. Controlled release scheduling."

"T8, release."

"T7, release."

"T6, release."

"T5, release."

I let go, close my eyes and throw my head back. Before the window opaques again, I strain around to try and see Pete in the greenhouse, but it's too far away, and I'm not fast enough to see more than a glimpse of green.

"T2, release."

"Handing over control to local T1 team."

"Orbit stable. All hands released. Mission complete."

I unbuckle and pull out of my cell. The others are drifting to their rooms. Exit isn't scheduled until tomorrow, so we've got a bit of time to prepare. Plus the T1s have to keep it steady for a while before Earth's feeling comfortable that it won't fall out of the sky.

A hand on my shoulder stops me before I can get any distance or speed up. "Wait up Indi, where you going in such a rush?" Tania.

"Nowhere. What's up?"

"How incredible was that? I can't believe we're responsible for pulling Titan to Earth."

Us being responsible is a stretch at best, but I nod anyway.

"I can't wait for the next one. I feel like I could go again right now. Have you signed up for Titania yet?"

I had, but Tania's words fill me with regret.

"Anyway, I'll be there. Hope we can room again. Some of the other Ts are getting together for a drink and party in the shaft before we hit land again. You wanna go?"

I pull away. "In a bit, I gotta do something first."

Escape. Back through the corridors, up the lift shaft, starting to fill with revelers, and up to Brandy and Michele again. A few short words with them that include staving off Brandy for yet another day, and then I'm in and searching for him again.

I find Pete surrounded by small white flowers on a bed of soft leaves, looking out over Earth's newest heavenly body. He smiles at me and blooms flowers in the canopy around his head. "I missed you," he says. "Titan looks beautiful in the sunlight."

"Not as beautiful as you," I say, kissing him softly as we sink into the cool green depths of his forest.

"Are you going with us to Titania?" Pete whispers as I undress him.

I nod.

"I'm glad. It wouldn't be the same without you."

About the Author

Adrik Kemp is an award-winning writer and author of horror, speculative fiction, and fantasy short stories and novels. He has short stories out in a number of publications, including *Pilcrow & Dagger, Aurealis Magazine, Transmundane Press, Torquere Press, Pride Publishing,* and *CSFG Press.*

*****~~~~~*****

New Heaven, New Earth

by Neil James Hudson

We reached the outermost star sphere four days after leaving the wormhole. I stood at the observation deck, looking for a sign. I could see no trace of the courses of the stars, no visible evidence of their spheres. But I seemed to see a greater ordering than I was used to. The bodies in front of me appeared to have been set in place deliberately, rather than the helpless results of random collisions.

I stood next to my First Officer Arya Laghani. I enjoyed her company and found her smart and efficient. I refused to find her attractive, though. The universe had changed, and it was futile to make attachments. "How long before we reach the Ptolemaic zone?" I asked.

"Two hours," she said. "I've informed the Bishop."

One of the stars before us had become a sun; still safe to look at, but noticeably brighter and larger than the others. "That outermost star has a system of eight planets," I said. "Except they no longer orbit it. They now orbit whatever is at the centre of this system. The same seems to go for their moons; they no longer orbit their planets. What's in the middle of it?"

"Our readings still suggest a planet. The innermost star is showing the same wobble we detected on Earth; it seems to be orbiting its planet, rather than the other way round. And everything else is focused on the same spot."

I heard the door open behind us, and turned to see Bishop Riesmann. He nodded to us both. "You still claim to have no faith, Tara?" he said to me.

"It would still be appropriate to refer to me as Captain."

"In the face of this?" He wore no uniform or insignia to portray his rank, instead wearing only the drab pale orange uniform that the rest of us used. "It's a strange feeling, to have been wrong all one's life; and yet, in a way, proven right."

"May I remind you, Bishop, that the geocentric system, for want of a better word, represents a severe existential threat to the human race. Since this phenomenon was discovered, it has been expanding at something near the speed of light, taking in everything it finds in its path; removing the laws of physics and replacing them with a Ptolemaic universe. It shows no sign of stopping. If it reaches our own solar system, the Earth will cease to orbit the Sun, and both will circle around some far more distant point. If we stay at the same distance, and the planet continues to rotate, we'll survive; we'll lose the seasons, but nature and our own technology will find a way. But if we orbit independently, we'll find ourselves moving further and further away from the Sun. Eventually, we're finished."

He shrugged. "No god would allow it."

Despite his importance to the mission, I found Riesmann irritating. "Religious considerations are the least of my worries."

"On the contrary; they have become everything."

"I'm busy," I said, and I left the deck to return to my cabin. But I knew that the Bishop was right. Back in history, when humanity had believed that the Earth was the centre of the universe, the religions followed logically; God lived in Heaven, watching us below, the most important things in the universe. Then Galileo dispelled the myth. The church had been right to suppress his work;

when we lost our special status, so did our gods, and religions jostled for position along with atheism and agnosticism. They weren't disproved, but neither was anything else.

Now they were disproved. There was an earth at the centre of the universe, around which all the heavenly bodies revolved. There was a god who moved the stars in their courses. But it wasn't our earth, it wasn't our god, and we were not part of the system.

We did not know now if the god even knew about us. We did not know if we had souls, or if we were walking meat that could be neither saved nor damned. Those of us who wished to pray had no idea who we were praying to. Those who wanted to live a good life had no idea what counted as sinful. The true religion had never been revealed to us.

Our mission was to find the planet at the centre of the universe, where Bishop Riesmann would petition the god to allow us in.

...

The Bishop had twelve acolytes, a superstitious number but one which he felt was necessary. They spent their days in prayer, trying to contact the new god, or at least alert him to our presence. The rest of us, myself excepted, were scientific and technical staff. As well as piloting the ship, they were here to find out as much about the phenomenon as possible. In particular, we needed to know what happened to solar systems when they were suddenly co-opted into the Ptolemaic universe. We needed to know what happened to planets.

I assembled everyone on board the vessel, both religious and technical staff. I asked Arya to explain our situation. She began by reading some figures from her tablet, which must have meant little to Riesmann and his followers. Then she explained.

"Our engines are firing, but they have no effect. We've now switched them off to conserve fuel. We are, however, still in motion. We appear to be in orbit around the new fixed point." She looked up from her tablet, watching for a reaction. "We have been set in a course around the centre, and we seem to be as unable to leave it as the stars and planets."

There was a brief silence. It was the Bishop himself who broke it.

"That must mean we have become part of the system; physically, if not theologically."

"That seems to be the case," said Arya.

"Then we may finally be at the stage where our prayers will be heard."

Arya looked to me. "This was always a prayer mission," I said. "And we always considered the possibility that we wouldn't be able to reach the planet. After all, geocentric models never allowed for meteorites; only divine agents were able to move further in."

A junior technician asked the question I didn't want. "What about moving out?"

"We have procedures in place. However, I will take no further action until Bishop Riesmann has been allowed to do his job."

I think they believed me because they wanted to. But an hour or so later, as I stood on the observation deck staring once more into the centre of the universe, Riesmann came and joined me.

"How bad is it?" he asked.

"We have supplies for some time yet," I said, not wanting to be specific.

"And when they run out?"

"You had better hope that the god shows mercy on us."

"And if he doesn't?"

"I think you are lacking in faith, Bishop."

"That is not an answer."

Heaven was not out here, I thought; it must have been on the new earth, the planet of souls in the middle of the universe. Its inhabitants knew they were special, that they could be saved by the divine. "We have supplies of a chemical toxin. Enough to place in our food. We will die painlessly, not of starvation."

"I see. And when do we decide to take this step?"

I turned to face him. I tried to read his face. I had no faith, but it didn't matter. The Bishop, however, needed all the faith he could find. The souls of billions might depend on him.

"I am the Captain," I said.

I watched as understanding dawned. "You'd make the decision? Our first contact with the god would end in murder?"

"Controlled suicide," I said. "Perhaps you should go back to your praying, Bishop. Only divine mercy can save us. Not just us; all of Earth."

He looked at me, horror still on his face. Then he set his expression, just as the stars had been set around the planet. He took on a seriousness, and a determination. He nodded, and left the room.

...

Riesmann and his acolytes spent all their waking time praying. As he himself said, they could be on the wrong frequency. He did not know if our traditional methods of prayer could be used to contact an unknown god. In the meantime I had my own job to do.

Bishop Riesmann was here to contact the god, but his previous faith could be a barrier to that. I had no faith; I was an empty vessel, waiting to be filled with the light of any deity with light to spare. I had been chosen for this mission precisely because of my agnosticism. I had no strong views on any religion.

I was to do everything within my power to convert to the new god.

I walked again to the observation room, looking out at the cosmos, the vast masses all orbiting the chosen people. I had always felt a little suspicious of religions, was rather pleased that I had not adopted one, not even atheism. I was now under orders to believe to my utmost ability.

I faced the new universe, and raised my arms. "Okay, god," I said. "Come and get me."

It wasn't enough to wait passively to be converted. I had tried that before. I had to actively give myself to the new god. Slowly, I let my heart fill with joy for my new lord. I gave myself over with love towards him. I accepted him as my one true saviour, pledged myself to his worship. I felt blessed in the knowledge of him.

I lowered my arms. This was fake. I saw no redemption in the centre of the universe. We would not be saved, would not be loved.

"I do not believe in you, god," I said out loud.

I heard a noise behind me and turned round. Arya stood in the doorway, an embarrassed look on her face. "What is it?" I asked.

She held her tablet out to me. I glanced at it, all thoughts of religious conversion forgotten.

"The planets are independent of their sun," I said.

She nodded. "The effect is still very small. As far as we can tell, the star and the planets are all orbiting at the same velocity. But their orbits are different sizes. Some of the planets are a little further in than the star; some a little further out. The system will break up."

"Thank you," I said.

"There's one other thing." She showed me some other readings.

"I don't understand."

"The chemical signature of one of the planet's atmospheres is completely wrong. It couldn't have evolved naturally."

"It's inhabited?"

"And it's giving off too much radiation. We can't find radio waves, but microwave radiation is far too high. We think it might be a post-industrial signature.

130

Congratulations, Captain. You've discovered intelligent life."

Which was being thrown away. If a god was ruling over the planet at the centre, no one else was invited to the party. "It might be best to keep this to ourselves," I said.

"Aye, aye, Captain."

"Actually, no." I thought again, wondering what would happen. Perhaps the god had taken possession of me after all, and I was unaware of the fact. "Tell Riesmann." Let him know the manner of the deity to which he prayed.

Arya nodded, and went to find the Bishop. I took one more glance at the new cosmos, then turned my back on it and its creator, and went to my cabin.

...

The only remaining question was when I should take the decision to terminate the mission, and poison our food.

We had supplies to last for three months. But long before that, everyone would know what was coming. We would know that the praying hadn't worked, that we were a doomed ship with no hope of escape. On the other hand, we had come here so that Riesmann could pray. I had to allow him time for his work. If I pulled the plug too soon, billions back home could die.

After three weeks of prayer, the alarm sounded to tell me that the airlock had been opened.

I knew immediately what must have happened. It was not a case of merely pressing a button or turning a handle. Only I had the authority to open it single-handedly, and even then two senior members of the crew could countermand the order if they felt it endangered the ship. If the airlock had been opened without my involvement, it must have taken nearly the entire crew.

I raced towards the hall, and found the entire crew waiting for me. The twelve acolytes stood aside from them.

"Where is Riesmann?" I shouted.

Arya handed me her tablet, on which a video began to play. It showed Riesmann's face; I watched as he spoke.

"There are three options, Captain," he said. "Perhaps we have no souls, and I am merely a robot who believes he is alive. If this is the case, my death is irrelevant.

"Or perhaps I have, in some way unknown to me, sinned against the new god. Perhaps I have not worshipped him correctly; perhaps I have committed some bizarre infraction of which we know nothing. I am aware that in my old faith, suicide itself was a sin. But this is a controlled one, no? I may, frankly, find myself in Hell. But again, if so, that must be my fate anyway. Postponing it by a few years would be pointless.

"But suppose I have lived a life of enough virtue and piety that even in the eyes of the god, I am one of the saved? Then I will ascend to Heaven, and take my place beside him. There, and only there, can I plead our case. I wonder if he will be surprised to see me? In any case, prayer has not worked, Captain. It may be a slim chance, but I must take it, and hope I can address the god in person.

"Should I fail, my only advice is to hope that the strictures of our great religions resemble those of the new one, and that we should all try to live a life of virtue. I therefore beg you, Captain, to remember that great virtue of forgiveness; and to use it on me."

The screen went blank. I looked up at the congregation before me, all expecting something of me.

It was time to terminate the mission.

And then some vast force threw me against the wall. Here there should have been no movement, no momentum, but it felt as if we were accelerating.

"What's going on?" I yelled, knowing that no one could possibly know.

132

Arya was frantically calculating. "We've left the orbit," she said. "We're being thrown out of the system."

"All the way out?"

She calculated some more. "We're travelling faster than the event horizon. We should be back in Galilean space in—" She looked down at the tablet, then looked back, unbelieving. "Hours?"

"Like we were swatted away," I said quietly.

One of the acolytes spoke up now. "The god has shown us mercy," he said.

And suddenly everyone in the room was shouting, cheering, embracing.

"Or rejection," I said, but no one seemed to hear.

...

I still see Arya. It is now six months since our return home. She told me yesterday that there was to be another prayer expedition. "From a safe distance, this time."

"Good luck to them," I said.

She looked at me, as if she were wondering if she could trust me. "They want to promote me. To lead the expedition. They want my knowledge of the new system."

"That's wonderful news."

"I want you to come as well. I need your experience."

I opened my mouth to refuse. I had had enough of gods. I had looked into the heart of the universe and found only darkness. I did not want to look a second time.

The Ptolemaic system isn't visible from the Earth; not yet. It takes our most delicate instruments to detect it. But it's coming. There is a plan to build space stations; to put them into orbit near the sun, at just the right time and just the right place that they will share its orbit. There is another plan to tap the geothermal energies beneath the Earth's crust, to provide heat and energy for the rest of us when the Sun has gone. Our species does not give up easily.

I thought of Riesmann, his body locked into its sphere around the planet of the god. Perhaps its inhabitants will detect him, wonder how he came to be there. I hope they give him a decent name, not just a catalogue number.

He failed, of course. I do not know if he met his god, but the Ptolemaic system is still coming, and will engulf us on its slow journey throughout the whole universe. If the god knew about us, or cared about us, he would have built a second system, with our world at the centre, and our own sun orbiting our own world. But I had looked at the centre of the universe and found no redemption, no love.

Did this mean there could never be love?

I found that I could not answer Arya. She had followed me almost to the centre of the universe, and I had nearly got her killed. But she was still here.

I felt as if I was looking at her for the first time. I realised she did not want me for my experience, and abruptly I felt as if I was in heaven.

"I'd love to come with you," I said.

About the Author

Neil James Hudson has previously published around forty short stories, including five for Third Flatiron ("The Mytilenian Delay" was shortlisted for a WSFA Small Press Award). His paranormal romance novel, *On Wings of Pity,* is available from Amazon, and his story collection, *The End of the World: A User's Guide,* can be ordered through his website at www.neiljameshudson.net. He lives in the UK, where he works as a charity shop manager.

*****~~~~~*****

First, They Came As Gods

by G.D. Watry

The priest just wanted to smoke a cigarette. But like the Earth's blue sky and the prickle of soft grass underfoot, that simple luxury was over 423 million miles away, on a planet that resembled nothing more than a pinprick in the black fabric of space. And in between, a vacuum. In these instances, when the priest's mind lingered on the distance, he craved simple pleasures: the scent of tobacco in his nostrils and the blooming warmth of the smoke in his lungs.

Instead, he settled for prayer.

He knelt in one of the Church of Io's pews and fished the Rosary from his coat pocket. The church was quiet. Lit candles flickered near the confessionals, where they were arranged like a miniature mute choir. The priest started running through the routine, the string of Hail Marys, followed by an Our Father. Lather, rinse, repeat. He rolled the Rosary's silicate rock beads between his fingers, pinching the edges.

Find peace, and you'll find home, the priest reminded himself.

He reached for it, that elusive quiet he used to find through prayer, but couldn't grasp it. Something changed. Over the years, resignation had crept into the priest's heart, and when he realized this, he thought a change of scenery might help rekindle his faith. He

135

thought he'd find meaning among the stars, but he only found emptiness and an alien environment ready to consume and destroy his body, the biological machinery specifically carved to fit Earth and nowhere else.

"*Our Father, who art in heaven,*
hollowed *be thy Name.*"

He murmured bastardized lines, wringing his clasped hands in frustration and impatience.

Now that he was away, the priest just wanted to go back to Earth. He missed the wind's kiss, the ocean's brush, and the forest's birdsong. The virtual reality chambers on Danube Station were poor substitutes for the real thing. Despite full immersion, the simulated experience never clicked with the priest. He couldn't suspend disbelief. Something that, he now cynically thought, should've been easy. He tried, but all he saw was technological trickery and sleight of hand. He wasn't on Earth. He was on Jupiter's moon Io, the most volcanically active body in the solar system.

"He talking to you yet?"

The familiar voice startled the priest. He hadn't heard the scientist open the heavy oak doors to enter the church. Based on her voice's volume, she was close in proximity. The priest glanced over his shoulder and saw her sitting a few rows back, legs propped up on the pew in front of her and fingers laced behind her head. A model of relaxation.

"We might get better results if you try it with me," the priest said, extending a hand.

The scientist scrunched her nose. "I gave that up a long time ago," she said. "Keep trying for the both of us, though."

The priest pushed back from the kneeler. "I was about to give up anyway." He angled himself towards the scientist, resting his legs on the pew's bench.

She wore the same wrinkled flight suit she always wore, the garment grimy, the insignia of The Cairn

Research Facility sewed into the breast pocket. Her soil-colored hair was tied up in a messy bun. The church's low light hid the freckles dotting the olive skin beneath her green eyes.

"Heard y'all found something," the priest said. He slipped the Rosary back into his coat pocket.

The scientist shifted her feet to the ground and leaned forward, as if about to whisper a secret. "Now, where did you hear that?"

The priest grinned. He had first met the scientist at one of the sparsely attended 6 p.m. Sunday masses. At the time, he was still one of Danube Station's greenest greenhorns. The scientist had stood at the back of the church, not participating in the mass, just watching. Since the Church of Io only attracted Danube Station's administrative employees, the priest had taken note of the scientist. He approached her after mass, and the resulting conversation ended up kindling a friendship, though the exchanges usually consisted of surface pleasantries and shop talk.

"Word travels fast around here," the priest said. "It's the talk of the mess hall."

"And what are they saying?"

"That The Cairn is about to announce the discovery of extraterrestrial life, that y'all are going to change how we view our place in the universe. Grandiose stuff like that. I bet everyone stationed on Europa will be pissed."

"They should've chosen fire over ice. Our theories were better," the scientist said. She pushed a strand of hair behind her ear. "Sounds like you've been talking to people from marketing."

"I shan't reveal my sources."

"Well, then I'll neither confirm nor deny your suspicions."

"Ah, come on," the priest sighed.

The scientist stood and exited the pew. She walked down the aisle towards the crucifix. The priest rose and followed, stopping where the scientist stood at the altar's edge.

The crucifix was a ghastly ornamentation. Christ's skeletal body and the cross were drizzled in molten iron from Io's core. The metal's weight caused the cross's horizontal axis to droop. Implosion looked imminent.

The scientist gazed beyond the crucifix and altar. Behind, a floor-to-ceiling window revealed Io's volcanic moonscape. "What do you see when you look out there?" she asked.

Danube Planum lay before them, with its rocky and explosive terrain. Ashy plumes bloomed from hollow vents, and lava rivers churned in gullies. Jupiter emerged from the dark alien sky, its giant unblinking eye—a storm of toxicity—staring down at them.

"An infernal Earth," the priest said.

"That's so Biblical of you."

"Well, I fit my appearance," he said, tugging on his clerical collar.

"No," the scientist said. She faced the priest, "You don't. You might play the part for your parishioners on Sunday, but that's all it is: a role. You might have your small flock fooled but not this black sheep. You're peddling a God you know isn't real."

"And what makes you think you know me so well?"

"You're like me," the scientist said. Her head lolled side-to-side, as if she was trying to stay awake. Her voice became thick, as if her tongue was molasses. "You're a searcher. And when something we seek isn't real, we don't stop seeking. We turn to other avenues, to other things to believe in. Rarely is there anything to be found in the tenets of organized religion. Its systems are too limiting."

It was hard for the priest not to take offense at that statement. Despite his internal bias, he winced when others criticized the faith he no longer subscribed to. He straightened his spine and raised his chin. "Is that why you came to Io? To find something?"

The scientist flashed a conspiratorial grin. "I already found it," she said, stepping closer to the priest and lowering her voice. "I'm here to spread the good news." She nodded once and returned her gaze to the moonscape beyond.

"So y'all did find something." The priest hadn't allowed himself to seriously consider the idea. Danube Station was small and insular. Often the rumors spreading around the station were just that, rumors. But this was different. This was revolutionary.

"That we did," the scientist replied. She raised her thumb to her mouth and chewed on the nail.

"Well, come on. Don't leave me in suspense here."

The priest thought he saw something in the scientist's body language, a subtle tremor that rolled wave-like over the entirety of her being. She appeared gaunt, her flight suit baggy and too big for her body. She fidgeted, a cap on a pressurized container.

"They're not like us," she said. "They thrive on our desperation for narrative and our search for coherence in a senseless universe." She swallowed deeply, as if the words she spat were more than she could chew. "Look at this place. A world of extremes. A place where temperatures range from 3,000 degrees Fahrenheit to negative 200. A place indifferent to our construct of life. Only the strongest survive here, and they've been waiting below the surface. Waiting for us to set them free and take them to other worlds, including ours."

The priest had heard that people on Danube Station sometimes experienced cabin fever. There was protocol to follow in such instances. "Insanity is catching," everyone on Danube Station learned during orientation. "If you see something out of the ordinary, report it. For the sake of the mission." The priest pocketed his right hand, rummaging around for the CommPilot.

The scientists shook her head. "That won't help."

The priest's finger hovered over the emergency call button, ready to press it. "If you don't want me to press it, you'd better start making sense."

The scientist blinked once, and by the time her eyelids lifted something had changed within her.

"How's this for making sense?" she said with her swollen tongue. "She was raised in the church, baptized without anyone considering that belief is an infliction, an expectation of something more beyond *this*. And for a while, she believed it. How could she not, through the lens of youth? But as she got older, she uncovered the lie, and she sought truth elsewhere. Just like you, she searched for it among the stars."

The priest's pulse quickened. His grip on CommPilot loosened.

"She found what she was looking for, priest," the thing inhabiting the scientist's body said. She knelt on the altar's steps. Another blink, and she was the scientist again. "We thought they'd live in frozen oceans and come to us in spaceships, but they live in lava tubes and travel through language. They sing a indifferent song that tells of destruction and rebirth, ad infinitum." She extended a hand to the priest. "I can tell you their story."

The priest knelt beside the scientist. He grabbed her hand and joined her in prayer.

After they finished, he helped spread the good news.

About the Author

G. D. Watry is a writer living in California. His work has appeared in *Hinnom Magazine, Pantheon*

Magazine, OCCULUM, Shotgun Honey, and *The Molotov Cocktail,* among other publications. You can find him on Twitter @GDWatry.

*****~~~~*****

And the Universe Waited

by Jo Miles

All day, she watched, while the others pretended not to. The micro-satellite's visual feed showed the progress on the ground: all according to schedule.

"Today," she said to whoever was listening. "It's going to happen today."

"It might be. . . ."

"But the Xylians have made mistakes before. . . . "

"There's so much that could go wrong. . . . "

The usual careful responses, armored with skepticism. As if they weren't checking the feed multiple times a minute, too. As if the rest of the ship, the rest of everyone everywhere across the Mesh, wasn't doing the same.

"It'll be today. They're going to do it." She leaned in toward the visual, where flea-sized creatures gathered around the launch pad, busy at work. Zooming in, she centered on a single Xylian, the project lead.

Lights flickered and shifted on the obelisk in the background, announcing updates in status where all team members could see them. The leader clustered in conversation with two of its team leads; it gesticulated with two of its sets of limbs, questions glowing and flickering across its iridescent torso. A translation floated across the display, but she'd learned to interpret the Xylian light-and-color language long ago. The leader was nervous, cautious by nature. Confident, but taking every precaution against another accident. This one was a good leader, clever, competent. One more reason why she was certain the Xylians would launch today.

It wanted another full systems check. She settled in to wait.

...

The old paradox: if life was so adaptable, if it could develop organically almost anywhere, under such a plethora of conditions. . . then where was everyone?

It baffled her ancestors, when they first reached the stars in their primitive ships. They scanned for signals, they sent out probes, and as their techniques advanced, they themselves searched. And with dawning dismay, they had to accept the truth: there was no one else.

They were alone.

Later, after an exhaustive search spanning thousands of Earth years, an amendment to that truth: Earth was not alone at the galaxy's party, but they had misread the invitation; they were mortifyingly early. All the intelligent life that their equations predicted? It hadn't finished evolving yet.

There was only one thing to do. They waited.

And they waited. On and on, through years, millennia, millions of years. They evolved patience, like the species they observed evolved versatile digestive systems and clever appendages and, sometimes, big brains.

The yearning was primordial. Ever since her ape ancestors first ground glass into lenses and built telescopes, since they discovered the nature of the planets, they had asked: are there others like us out there? And before that, long before, when *their* ancestors first dropped down from the trees and faced the vastness of their own small world, since the earliest language first found a word for "alone," that was something no one wanted to be. Not in the long run.

And so, they took to the galaxy. Through their fiery and self-destructive adolescence, when they couldn't even take care of our own world, they grasped for the stars and dreamed of adventures on other worlds with aliens who talked and thought like them. Earth survived into their maturity, and the species spread, and spread, and spread. A slow and lonely journey: mapping the galaxy, terraforming and colonizing and falling back, littering the stars with the ruins of their species, relics for some far-future visitors to find. Seeking out, one by one, each naturally life-bearing planet and settling in to watch.

To wait.

(Today she was incapable of waiting. Today, anticipation made the seconds crawl like millennia. She zoomed in on the feed again. Some sort of hold-up. A faulty part. Replacements being sought. More delay. Risk of postponement.)

This was the scope of her species' patience: what matter if it took a million years to reach a distant world, if it might take that planet's primordial beings 600 million years to evolve enough to say hello? Their own species might evolve (and had evolved) into something unrecognizable in that time, as foreign as an ape to a trilobite, but the longing for company never faded. If they watched and waited and studied and perhaps even nurtured—if they went so far as to deflect a devastating asteroid, or nudge the climate in a direction more favorable to rapid evolution—and if they did this on a million worlds, eventually they would be rewarded.

Fortunately for her species, fortunately for her, the numbers were not that dire. They found thousands of planets with a head start on those 600 million years. Dozens with a considerable head start. Her own homeship set out only seventeen million years ago for Xy.

145

Recently, for the past 10,000 years or so, the question to bet on was which of these favored planets would yield intelligence first. Or better, which would first travel to space? Would even their most promising subjects evolve enough to begin a conversation?

Ever since she was a child, she was certain that this one would. The atmosphere on Xy was thick and storm-prone. Clouds obscured ninety percent of the sky at any given moment. But the other ten percent. . . She had always believed those rare glimpses of stars would prove as tantalizing to the clever, curious Xylians as Earth's moon had proved to her own distant ancestors.

Wishful thinking, the Mesh responded to her theories. *Your homeship orbits Xy. You wish them to succeed because you dream you'll be there when it happens. Do you know how many have lived and died with the same dream? More than there are cells in your body. The best you can hope is that one of your descendants may see that day.*

But if millions of generations hadn't embraced that dream, she would not be here now, and some generation had to be the one to see the dream fulfilled. Why not hers? Maybe she entered the xenobiologic service with childish dreams of glory, but over 400 Earth-years of study had given her solid reasons for confidence in them. Swaths of Xylian art, literary recordings, theater, devoted to the holy mysteries of space. Their technological advances, evident even from high orbit: a planetary communications network, high-atmosphere transportation. The exuberance with which they seized and examined each new bit of space debris that survived passage through their atmosphere—including those that she planted herself, gentle nudges toward the stars. She knew.

It would not be her distant descendants who made contact. It might be her children. It might be her.

It might be today.

While the Xylians built toward this moment, their progress growing so obvious that no one could ignore it, her own people echoed the same questions again and again through the Mesh: *Are they ready? What would it have done to us, at their age, to know for a fact we were not alone?* But at last the debate subsided to consensus. *Yes, they must be ready. We must not become so comfortable in the act of waiting that it eclipses our goal. They are ready, and so are we.*

...

Engines roared to life.

Rocket engines. Combustive propulsion, like the very first ships to leave Earth. For some reason, that detail choked her up. Across such vastness: rocket engines.

Motion on the display. The rocket hefted from its platform. The feed shifted its angle, keeping the ship centered as it climbed.

"Unh—"

A sharp breath from her colleagues—from all her species, giving up the pretense of doubt or indifference. She found the problem on the display: the indicator for attitude, careening. Like the ship careened, maddened, as if trying to shake off its own engines.

A load-balancing error. Such an idiotic reason for failure, far too trivial a problem to avalanche into full disaster. . .

But no, not trivial to a people who'd never built a rocket before.

"Please," she whispered to the display. "Fix it."

Gravitational forces on the cabin neared her estimates of the Xylians' physical upper limits. Torque on engine connectors in the danger zone and rising.

A piece broke free, tumbled away too fast for visual identification. She moved to scroll back the feed and zoom in on the object, but the status display caught her attention. Indicators still moving, but slowing. Attitude stabilizing.

The rocket continued on its way.

"Well done," she said, and sat back to watch. Analysis could wait for later.

...

The Xylians broke atmosphere.

For the first time, they reached space. From her simulations, she knew what they experienced: bone-grinding turbulence, giving way to shocking, perfect stillness. And the best view of the stars they'd ever seen.

The microsatellite intercepted their transmissions, routed them to the display. All systems check.

She looked around at her colleagues, found them riveted with spiritual anticipation. All agreed, breathless: it was time for the next step.

The homeship moved into high but visible orbit above the rocket's position, pulsing a message for all to see:

Hello.

...

Then: the longest wait of all.

Her people had spent millennia preparing for this day. Nervous as they were, they knew precisely what to do, had a plan for every contingency. Not so for the Xylians. Of course they had asked themselves, as her people had: *Are we alone?* But in all the scenarios surrounding this launch, they never dreamed of this one.

The crew of the rocket never expected to be ambassadors. They had no authority to decide their course of action. They could only report: *this ship, massive, out of nowhere. A single message, a greeting. No sign of hostility.*

On the ground, in closed rooms, beyond the reach of her monitoring equipment, politicians and bureaucrats, scientists and generals debated what to do.

There were several courses open to them, all well-documented and analyzed and planned for by her ancestors, their statistical likelihood calculated. The

148

Xylians might ignore the homeship: possible, but unlikely. They might decide to wait and study this astonishing visitor in their sky: the most prudent course. They might well panic and launch a military response: no physical danger to the homeship, but devastating to her species' hopes.

Or. . .

It happened a whole Xylian day later. A full day of argument and unanswerable questions. Then the rocket rotated along its axis, baring its belly to the stars. Indicator lights came to life, pulsing out a primitive code:

Hello. We see you.

###

About the Author

Jo Miles is a graduate of the Viable Paradise writers workshop. She has fiction published in *Diabolical Plots* and the *Agents and Spies* anthology.

*****~~~~~*****

The Bright and Hollow Sky

by Martin M. Clark

Waiting.

One ship, hiding in the rings of a gas giant, on minimum power, silent as the grave. A speck in the firmament, overlooked even by God.

After seven months of combat the *Helel* was all that could be spared to cover the evacuation of Magdalene Station, an orbital gas mine in the Andora Reach system. Our usual battle rider frigates had been replaced by multiple missile pods, but even given this massive increase in firepower we were one light cruiser against an anticipated attack force in the hundreds.

Our enemy called themselves "The Dream"—we knew nothing more about them. They killed every human being they encountered. They ignored all attempts at diplomacy, pleas for mercy, offers of surrender. Their damaged ships blew themselves up rather than risk capture. All we could do was fight, retreat and fight again—attrition as non-verbal communication.

Except that no one was listening.

...

Illumination on the bridge was minimal. The other crew members were just bulky shapes of light and shadow in the warm glow of electronics, anonymous in armoured vac suits. The Dream strike craft carried a needle-point mass-driver; a smaller version of the spinal mount aboard our battlewagons. Against this we had virtually no defence and penetrating hits were anticipated.

"Possible jump point detected, Captain. Sector seven-fifteen-three, system relative."

The voice startled me; despite being too wired to rest I'd sunk into a contemplative doze. I cleared my throat and returned to the here-and-now. "You'll have to do better than that, Miss Hughes, 'possible' won't cut it, I'm afraid."

I could almost hear her blush with embarrassment. "Sorry sir, awaiting confirmation and triangulation from station sensors and source Alpha."

"Carry on."

I brought up the system schematic on my helmet display, looking for any way to improve our tactical situation. The station was protected by a smattering of proximity mines plus a few short-range gun platforms. We were in the optimum ambush position, assuming the Dream didn't approach from the far side of the sun. Not that they were likely to try a sneak attack, but at least my back was covered by an improvised sensor net.

"Confirmation received, Captain." Excitement tinged her voice. "The distortion effect indicates a Dream warship, assault carrier class."

Pretty much what I'd expected, but it would be nice to be wrong sometimes. "Very well. Comms, alert Magdalene Station. Micro-burst, tight-band. XO?"

"Sir?" Vought turned a blank helmet visor in my direction.

"Prepare for main engine restart."

"Reactor to standby, aye, sir."

I took a deep breath. "Arm and load all nuclear weapons."

"I concur, Captain. Voiceprint identification and contextual analysis has been confirmed. Nuclear protocol is in effect."

And after that brief flurry of activity. . . we waited.

Not that long, though, indicating the artificial wormhole created by their carrier was linked to a near-by system. Close, but no cigar; still no hint as to their base of operations and the semi-mythical 'command carrier' Fleet Intel was so desperate to find.

"Distortion wave detected. Long-range telemetry from Magdalene Station estimates two-hundred-plus enemy ships have emerged from the wormhole. Estimated time to optimal firing point. . . seventeen minutes."

"Thank you, Miss Hughes. Helm, take us up above the rings. Slowly now. "

That wasn't strictly necessary, as we'd be able to track the incoming ships via remote sensors until one side or the other was destroyed. But I wanted to see them, the enemy, if only this once.

The swarm of Dream strike craft were back-lit by one of the several other gas giants in the system. A great cloud of dark-grey ships, constantly changing formation as they surged towards the station, like a swirl of ink thrown into still water. A stain to blot out humanity.

I shifted uncomfortably in my chair, the combination of fatigue and stimulants making by bones ache. "Bring main power on-line. Active sensors. Light them up, Miss Hughes, I want confirmation of that carrier's position. Mister Vought?"

"Sir."

"Commence missile launch as soon as telemetry is received." I flicked to ship-wide transmission. "All hands, this is the Captain. We have engaged the enemy and can expect their close attention. Secure all stations and set condition one throughout the ship. This is no drill. Captain out."

"Pod launch sequence underway, Captain."

"Thank you, Mister Vought. Ready single ship-to-ship missile for firing."

That was niggardly, I know, but we'd received notification from the Admiralty not to expect any further resupply from fleet tenders. The euphemistic "local resources" would have to do from now on.

"Confirmed, sir. Single ship-to-ship missile ready for firing. Designation is N-One."

"I want a ten-second gap between the last pod launch and N-One. I want it tucked in close behind the shoal, as neat as you can manage. Do—"

"Sir!"

"Miss Hughes?"

"Some ninety enemy craft have broken formation and are heading in our direction."

Damn, but that was quick. I'd counted on sensor backwash from the gas giant to hide the launch at least until our missiles cleared the rings. Still, it wasn't their entire force and I hoped a fair proportion would double back to protect the carrier when the real target became apparent.

"Mister Vought?"

"The shoal missiles are in deadfall mode, ETA with target is eleven minutes twenty seconds. Telemetry signal strength is strong, and we have achieved a ninety-three percent launch rate. Our N-One missile is in stealth mode and the chance of its detection is minimal."

"Enemy reaction?"

"An *additional* fifty to sixty strike craft have broken off from the main formation and are vectoring towards our missiles. Based on the estimated position, course, and speed of our ordnance, I'd say the Dream will intercept in approximately four minutes ten seconds. Still way outside the effective range of a strike on the carrier. Orders?"

So much for divide and conquer. I badly wanted to drum my fingers on the arm of my chair but the armoured gauntlets made that too laboured and awkward. Instead I took a deep breath of antiseptic air and scanned the tactical overlay.

"What's the enemy intercept effectiveness? The second squadron."

Vought paused, obviously running a scenario projection through tactical analysis. "They're playing catch-up, of course, but I estimate less than fifteen percent of our missiles will reach the enemy carrier. However, of a more immediate concern is the remaining enemy force, which will be within firing range in under two minutes."

"Very well, deploy counter-measures, maximum spread."

"Sir."

Our point-defence guns were designed to engage conventional missiles at close range. As such they were well-nigh useless against the hyper-velocity kinetic rounds used by the Dream. However we'd switched to a fragmentation load, thus generating a wall of debris between us and the enemy. Laser range-finding would be rendered useless by the chaff, reducing both sides to manual targeting, except that *we* still had external telemetry from the surveillance net.

"All batteries firing, sir."

Plus I had an Ace up my sleeve.

Well, if not exactly an Ace then definitely a Joker—fresh out of the R&D labs on Tigris. It was officially "experimental"—a polite way of saying they'd be pleasantly surprised if the damn thing worked under battlefield conditions. Not something I'd wanted to use if it could possibly be avoided, but the odds were just too heavily stacked against us.

My mouth was dry. "Mister Vought, prepare and load Hellhound missile." It's one thing to set an attack dog on someone, quite another to unleash a slavering, rabid beast with an indiscriminate appetite.

He hesitated, then accessed the restricted ordinance subsystem. When Vought spoke, there was a hint of relief in his voice. "Initiation successful and containment is holding steady. We have an estimated three minutes fifteen seconds before magnetic dissipation."

"Immediate launch."

One and two and three and. . .

"Missile away, Captain. Designation is H-One."

"Point defence, cease fire. Helm, bring us about. Reciprocal course to H-One, all ahead full."

"Helm responding, sir. All ahead full, aye. Captain, we're heading directly into the gas giant."

"Thank you Mister Kurtz, I'm well aware of that."

Normally I would have chewed him out for questioning an order on the bridge—not even Vought was afforded that privilege—but I was concentrating on the Hellhound as it powered towards the Dream. I switched the bridge screen to directly aft, where the enemy ships were now showing as small specs in open space; a shoal of fireflies.

"H-One closing on target. Time to optimal deployment thirty-five seconds. . . Thirty seconds. . . Twenty-five. . . Twenty seconds."

"Come on, come on." I found I was whispering to myself, "Just a little further."

An unseen shot from a Dream ship struck H-One. Magnetic containment failed, allowing the eight segments of Dark Matter to collapse inwards, forming a Hawking sphere. Mass became energy became *other*.

A micro-singularity, a black hole.

The heart of the Hellhound.

Oblivion beckoned, and everything followed, even light itself.

I stared into the abyss.

The *Helel* shuddered.

"Sir, all forward movement has ceased. We're being drawn backwards."

I snapped out of my ghastly revere. "Mister Kurtz, all ahead flank. Miss Hughes, what's happening out there?"

"We've lost all external telemetry, sir. Gravitational distortion makes it impossible to tell what effect this is having on the enemy."

"Answering all ahead flank, sir." Kurtz sounded jittery. "Captain! We're still moving backwards, but forward sensors indicate we're *also* closing on the gas giant. It's, it's coming at us."

I gripped my chair arms, feeling the ship trembling beneath me, even through my suit. "Mister Vought. Anything left in the engines?"

"Currently at one-two-one percent of safe operational maximum. At this rate there won't be anything left *of* the engines in about two minutes."

I could see ring material streaming past us into nothingness. If this went on much longer it would be followed by the gas giant's upper atmosphere. God knows what long-term effect that would have on orbital stability but that was the least of my concerns.

Miss Hughes spoke, her voice a high-pitched squeak. "Captain! The local event horizon is collapsing!"

"Helm, prepare to cut engines on my command."

"Cut engines, sir?"

"Yes, cut engines on my command, Mister Kurtz. We won't be needing them much longer."

One way or another.

"Captain, radiation output from the singularity is increasing exponentially. Wavelength is approaching the visible spectrum."

A conventional black hole could swallow any amount of matter, but not our transient singularity. Choke it, and the gravimetric incline would invert, violently. Resulting in. . .

The visual flared and cut off as light intensity overloaded the external sensors; a micro *white* hole filled the screen. The *Helel* leapt forward, acceleration overwhelming internal gravity and pressing me back into

157

my chair. "Full reverse. Dammit, Kurtz, full reverse, *now!*"

Vought grabbed hold of the ops table with both hands. "Shock wave approaching. All hands, brace for impact."

I felt the ship twist, and someone cried out "emergency braking," but I couldn't tell if it was me or Kurtz or the Archangel Gabriel himself. Then a breeze tickled my skin, and my head was filled with a jumble of images; places, people—some long gone, some I didn't recognise. The disorientation was like a mild hallucinogenic. Not so much a distortion of reality but more a case of fixating on commonplace events and finding them endlessly funny. I giggled, I laughed, I roared until my jaws ached, I screamed.

I blinked.

We were intact, the crew at their posts, stirring or already checking systems. External visual had returned and was again white, but not the searing maw of a singularity inversion, more a swirling milky mist. From that I guessed we'd entered the gas giant's atmosphere but thankfully come to a halt before pressure crushed our hull. I took yet another stimulant as a guard against unhelpful thoughts and tried to speak, but my throat was so dry that all that came out was an inarticulate croak. I drank from my suit, until the "refill" light came on and the world seemed a more manageable place.

"Mister Vought, status?"

"Captain. The ship is answering "all stop" with engines on standby. Our current position is some 2,000 metres inside the atmospheric boundary. The hull is intact. Most primary systems are functioning, although we sustained damage to our forward targeting array and attitude jets; in fact the whole bow took quite a beating from impacts with ring matter." He straightened up and came to attention, or as far as his suit would allow. "I declare the ship fit for active duty, and we await your command."

"Thank you. Helm, take us up. Ready weapons."

There was no discernible movement. The atmosphere simply thinned like fog on the breeze, and suddenly we were in clear space again.

"Miss Hughes, kindly re-establish our data links. Mister Vought, do we have company?"

"I'm not detecting any survivors of the force that engaged us, sir."

"And the bad news?"

"The station is under attack and will be overwhelmed before we can intervene. The loss will be total."

I sighed. "That was always going to be the end result, regardless. Status of our missile strike?"

"Sorry, sir, but my best guess is the Dream interception force will catch up sooner rather than later. We're still tracking them, but the telemetry from Magdalene Station is spasmodic at best. And we've lost input from source Alpha, whatever it was."

There was blood in my mouth, but I resisted the temptation to spit in case the suit couldn't cope. I felt cold and tired, the backs of my eyes itchy, my back slick with sweat. I straightened up. "Mister Vought, bring N-One to a halt. Set warhead to proximity detonation, maximum sensitivity."

And stand well back.

He hesitated for a moment, then obviously realised what I was attempting. "Confirmed." There was a smile in his voice, even through my helmet speakers.

I wanted to rub my eyes and down a double espresso in lieu of sleep, but reality has this unpleasant habit of running things to its own timetable.

A warning light pulsed on the console in front of us.

"Nuclear detonation confirmed, Captain. . . Analysis of the blast indicates it's in the anticipated 400-megaton range."

The blast and electro-magnetic pulse should have fried a fair number of the enemy, while hopefully leaving our inert ordnance unscathed. Crippling the assault carrier would maroon their attack craft—and the Dream never came looking for survivors.

"Prepare to launch a second. . . " I trailed off, distracted by a new flashing alert. I echoed it to Vought.

"Sir? It's a stellar event notification, from one of the in-system surveillance drones. We couldn't secure a full complement of intelligence hardware and had to make do with some generic survey kit, so I placed them in less sensitive areas. Probably just a solar flare."

Probably just a solar flare, but I could feel apprehension crawling up my spine. "Mister Vought, be so kind as to indicate the positions of our probes on the main display."

The system sprang into 3-D view, with small pulsing green dots indicating the network of drones between the station and sun. I gestured towards those closest to the solar body. "Look, those two, *three*, there have gone black, indicating a loss of signal."

"Well, sir, it could be some form of enemy attack on our intelligence grid, I suppose. It's too widespread to be the result of a solar event." But I could hear the doubt in his voice.

Four, five, six blackspots on the image.

Rumours and scuttlebutt, they circulated at flag level just as they did amongst the swabbies. I'd heard hints of a thermo-stellar weapon, a game-changer; a weapon that could supposedly obliterate an entire Dream fleet.

And a spook ship, "source Alpha," hidden in the solar glare.

My heart went cold. "That's no electronic attack, that's a massive coronal ejection! Mister Vought, restore

160

full power and prepare to jump the ship. Helm. Bring us about, destination, ah, destination zero-zero-zero, absolute."

I could almost feel the ripple of hesitation run round the bridge. Vought tried to keep his voice low. "Captain, we're too close, too deep in the gravity well."

"Helm!"

"Helm answering, sir, she's coming about. Course laid in."

Still Vought hesitated, indecision plain in his body language, even under the vac suit.

"Mister Vought!"

"FTL hardspin, aye, sir! Single jump, Sol system."

My clenched fingers tore padding from the chair arms. "Rescind reactor fail-safes. Take everything she's got."

Seven, eight, nine. The sun had gone nova—the ultimate weapon in a game of attrition.

"Capacitor supercharger on line. Jump field forming. . . Jesus, the distortion, I've never seen—"

"*Now*, Vought, *now!*"

Reality side-slipped, revealing a universe of mass and magic; the gas giant a yawning pit beneath us, the stars black coals in a sea of shimmering light.

We jumped.

We flew.

We soared across the bright and hollow sky.

We twisted.

We tumbled.

We fell.

...

To Earth.

Tunguska, Siberia, on the morning of 30 June 1908.

The blast obliterated 2,000 square kilometres of forest.

I regained consciousness, alone, in an escape pod designed for six crewmen—with no memory of how I came to be here.

My head hurt.

To the local peasants I was just a crazy man who stumbled out of the forest. Although I had a smattering of Russian from my time aboard the Red Banner orbital, it took weeks to piece together the "where"—and "when." I was marooned, centuries before my time. I didn't even have enough knowledge of Earth history to become a credible soothsayer.

So I stayed, a stranger in a strange land. Tilling the fields in return for a meal and a place to sleep, avoiding the local authorities. The villagers think I'm an escaped criminal, but the ultimate prison is always hope. For if the *Helel* could leap across the years then perhaps others will follow. So on clear nights I sit and watch the sky, hoping to spot movement against the stars.

Because my future is still out there.

Waiting.

About the Author

Martin Clark is from Dumfries, in southwest Scotland. He's the author of supernatural noir novellas, originally published by Eggplant Literary Productions. Martin's first novel, *Whisper My Name,* is available on Kindle from Amazon. He's also had short stories published in other Third Flatiron anthologies and e-magazines such as *Nebula Rift* (now *Storyteller*), *Timeless Tales, Kraxon Magazine,* and *Mythaxis.*

*****~~~~~*****

GRINS & GURGLES

Devouring the Classics: Ten Recipes

by Rachel Rodman

Sphinx Stew
In the morning:
    Set broth to boil in a large cauldron.
    Add four lion legs.
In the afternoon:
    Add two eagle wings, plucked.
    Lower heat to simmer.
In the evening:
    To the thickened broth, add three human heads.
    Liquefy.

Cerberus Kombucha
3 dog heads, severed
Ferment in darkness.

Beware of Greeks Bearing Casseroles
Inside of a glass baking dish, set
    2 layers of lasagna
    1 layer of shrapnel and nitroglycerin
    2 additional layers of lasagna
Set timer for midnight.
Sprinkle with Trojan condoms.

Mediterranean Playboy
1 small bull
1 large eagle
1 large swan
Chop fine.

Marinate meat, 3-5 hours, in a concentrated solution of STDs: herpes, chlamydia, and so on—enough for a god.

Cook well.

Sauce (optional): 3 parts ambrosia, 1 part personal lubricant.

Labyrinth Beef
1/2 bull carcass, divided precisely along the mid-line

Snarl cooking twine over meat, 7 layers thick, knotting over and under, over and under, until your fingertips begin to bleed, and a feeling of profound dislocation begins to overwhelm you.

Broil.

While the beef cooks, and once you have bandaged your wounds, you may consider attempting to recover your equanimity via vigorous sex with some sort of farm animal.

Bacchus Cocktail
2 goat legs
Let soak in wine, one full course of the sun.

Using the wine-soaked legs like cudgels, bash in the brains of 1 or more police officers.

Collect the spray, mid-gush, in a cocktail glass.

Between sips, swirl it, O, swirl it!— human blood, mixed with goat meat, mixed with wine, wine, wine.

Laugh maniacally.

Arachne's Soufflé

Start with all of the usual ingredients—I won't demean you by enumerating them.

Stir and shape, whip and bake until it is utterly gorgeous. And transcendentally exquisite. And incomparably perfect.

Far better, that is, than anyone else, anywhere, might ever aspire to: any celestial beings, too, who might be listening in, *very pointedly included.*

Mock Heaven, between bites.

Pair with a postprandial cocktail: spider legs, spider cephalothoraxes, and assorted wisps of spider silk, suspended in tarantula tequila.

Gorgon with Gorgonzola

12 snakes, chopped in half, then left to writhe, writhe, writhe on a stone platter, until they are forever still

Dress with blue-veined cheese.

Cronus Popcorn

This is a no-frills recipe, predating the pretensions of all of those fancy cooking schools. And possibly a little rougher than anything you are accustomed to.

There are 2 steps.

    1) Gather together all of your children.

    2) Eat them.

Chew or don't chew, as you care to. Salt and butter, or not.

There is only one critically important component to this recipe. And, really, *I cannot emphasize this enough*:

You must be certain to eat ALL of them.

The Founding of Rome

Two wolf pups, deboned

Slow roast for 1 day.

###

About the Author

Rachel Rodman writes fairy tales, food poetry, and popular science. Her work has appeared in *Fireside Fiction, Daily Science Fiction, Expanded Horizons,* and elsewhere.

*****~~~~*****

No Encore

by Ville Nummenpää

During all my years as a professional harpsichordist, there was one event that defined me as an artist. I have never shared this with anyone until now. Come, let me take you there.

November 5, 1983, The Royal Smithsonian Hall. Capacity 2500. That's 2500 seats waiting to be filled, because of yours truly. Surely my biggest concert up to date. Little was I to know that the evening would end in horror and bloodshed.

I don't recall being nervous, but I do remember the sensation that hit me onstage. Pure adrenaline. Raw, untamed energy. Something I hadn't felt before, or haven't since.

It all started very well, with all limbs intact, all major organs firmly inside my body. I was on fire, you might say. To the extent that, halfway through Mozerto's 2nd opus, I broke a string. Not just any string, it was the dreaded high C. How to play 2nd Opus without high C you ask? Impossible? Exactly what I would have said up until that point. However, at times like these you learn to cope with the impossible. And that is exactly what I did. I kept on playing.

However, as the surge of adrenaline peaked, an unwelcome need to sneeze overcame me. As I sneezed, my liver exited my body through the nostrils. I couldn't believe it. There it was. My liver, splat across the precious notes, handwritten by Mozerto himself in 1765! I had violated the first rule of show business: *Always keep your liver inside the body!*

Determined not to break the second rule, I decided the show would go on. Oh yes it would. If I could only make it to the *libresse* just after the *socco vote minore*, I could grab my liver with my left hand, and snort it back in. . .

Destiny had planned something else for me.

Having memorized the demanding piece, I really didn't need the notes. Therefore, the bloody organ smudging the notes before me did not disturb my performance one bit. What did, was the fact that my right arm fell out of its socket just before I was about embark on a wild fluctuating ascend across the keyboard in a furious frenzy.

It made an audible thump hitting the ground, but there was surprisingly little gushing of blood from the recently vacated socket. Possibly due to the high amount of experimental antihistamine I had indulged in before the show—we shall never know. I also made a mental note of the remarkable absence of gasps and cries of horror emanating from the audience, but I could not let such a trivial detail bother me at that point.

As we all know, Mozerto's 2nd is a physically demanding piece. There are few, if none, harpsichordists in the world who could execute the nearly impossible *regatos* and *vigorettes* Mozerto had written in violent spouts of creative turmoil, or let alone, elaborate such difficult sentences as this one, witnessed now by yourself, brought to you by yours truly, at this very moment.

But I did. By God, I did.

To put it bluntly, at this point I had nothing to lose. An incident like this would surely bring down anyone's career, so the only thing left for me was to go out with a bang. I did, indeed, finish the concert. And predictably, nearing the end, my left arm also fell off.

I hardly even noticed. Such was my determination at that point, that I simply concluded Mozerto's 2nd Opus using only my forehead. I even managed the dreaded *arpeggio* in the climax, and finished the piece in triumph. Liverless, and armless.

There was silence. Was it awe, or a shared feeling of unease amidst the crowd? Either way, there was no applause. In a manner of self-taught dignity, I walked to the edge of the stage and took a deep bow. This was when they turned on the lights. . .

No one. There was not a soul in the audience. Not a single seat was occupied by an appreciative lover of the finer arts.

Embarrassed, but unfazed, I quickly re-stuck my arms back in their respective sockets, and snorted my liver back through the nostrils. Not letting the Smithsonian staff witness my discomfort, I simply left the building and took a taxi to the nearest emergency clinic.

It was only later in the hospital that I learned my career wasn't over. I was informed that, had the press been present, they would have reviewed my performance as "relentless," or as a "triumph over disaster." And had there been anyone in the audience, they surely would have been entertained by what they would have witnessed.

Ironically, it was the lack of audience, the very fact that no one cares at all about harpsichordists, that saved me from embarrassment, and allowed my career to soar to levels of unequalled mediocrity in the end.

About the Author

Ville Nummenpää is a screenwriter and a playwright by trade and writes short stories for fun. He gets some published on occasion, and is genuinely surprised on each occasion.

Ville believes there is only one thing in life worth taking seriously, humor.

*****~~~~~*****

Just Right Guy

by Art Lasky

Just Right Guy is the ideal superhero. Most super heroes are too much or too little to be interesting. What do I mean? Consider: Superman, too damn super. He is so powerful that he can solve any problem and defeat any villain, in a matter of seconds.

Now, what's his name, the Bat's, a wimp; he's just one slip or one unlucky bullet away from death. A real supervillain would eat him for breakfast. I think he's really an anonymous per diem worker. My bet is that Alfred's the real power behind the throne, he's on Bat number 732 (465 dead, the rest disabled). I'm sure well-written nondisclosure agreements keep that franchise alive.

Anyway, getting back to Just Right Guy, JR as he is known to his friends. He can't leap a tall building in a single bound. A medium-sized building with a good running start and the wind at his back is about the best he can manage. Faster than a speeding bullet? Well, maybe in a sprint, you know, thirty to forty yards or so, as long as it's not shot from a high-powered rifle. You get the picture: a good mid-range super hero, with just enough power to make it interesting. Let me tell you my favorite JR story.

JR was relaxing on the patio of his Fortress of Solitariness, located near the North Pole—North Pole,

New York, that is—when the call came in. Luth Lexar had just escaped from the Maximum Security Wing of the Prison for Super Smart Psychopaths and Tele-evangelists. JR leapt into action, racing to Luth's not overly secret hideout at a respectable 45 miles per hour.

By the time he arrived, it was too late; the evil genius faced JR with a sneer in his voice.

"Ha! Ha! Ha! You're too late Just *Wrong* Guy, I've used my attract-o ray to draw a giant asteroid toward the Earth. In a few hours this planet will be smashed to bits, and your puny powers are not enough to prevent it."

With that, Luth Lexar held out his hands and continued speaking.

"Go ahead, take me back to prison. I want to spend Earth's last hours gloating in my cell."

JR, being morally ambivalent and not at all concerned with due process, tore both of Luth's arms off and left him to bleed to death. With one almost-mighty bound he leapt to the phone. He dialed his friend's private number.

"Hi, Clarke, it's me JR, how're you doing?. . . How's Loise?. . . Yeah, we're both fine, thanks for asking. Look, I need a little favor; there's an asteroid hurtling toward the Earth. . . Ha, yeah, these supervillains are pathetically predictable. . . . You'll take care of it?. . . Great, thanks. Right, I'll see you at the Friday night poker game, bring plenty of money with you, ya big loser. . . . Give it up, Super *Tell* Man. . . . In your dreams. . . Okay, later, 'tater."

With that he headed back to the Fortress of Solitariness, pausing only to stomp Luth Lexar's body to be sure he was dead.

###

About the Author

Art is a retired computer programmer. After forty years of writing in COBOL and Assembler he decided to try writing in English; it's much harder than it looks. He lives in New York City with his wife/muse and regularly visiting grandkids. You can contact him at: ALASKY9679@YAHOO.COM.

*****~~~~~*****

Advice for the 2060s Birder

by Lisa Timpf

It's that time of year again, when citizen scientists across the world—what's left of it, anyway—venture forth to count, catalogue, and report bird species they encounter. If you're planning to participate in the 2061 Backyard Bird Count, you've come to the right place for the latest advice.

Since so many scientists were lost in the most recent wave of nuclear devastation, the efforts of ordinary citizens such as you is more vital than ever! Perhaps, as you look out your half-melted windows at the yellow-brown vegetation and the leaden skies above, you may be tempted to sink into despair. But, fear not! Birding may not be quite what it was in your parents' day, or for that matter, earlier in your day, but there is still plenty of fun to be had.

Before you head out on count day, I suggest that you equip yourself with the updated *U Name It* bird app, except in those areas (all too plentiful, alas) where internet coverage has not yet been restored. In these locations, you may want, barbaric as it sounds, to pack a printed bird guide, ideally of recent enough vintage to include some of the mutated species. Binoculars are, of course, a must, and a Geiger counter is highly recommended.

This year, record levels of buzzards, vultures, crows, and other carrion-eaters are expected, given recent events. In most areas, robins, blue jays, starlings, and the like might still be spotted, although count participants are asked to make a note of any extra limbs, misshapen beaks, or third eyes.

The myriad mutations keep things interesting, although squabbles persist on the fringes of academia regarding whether, for example, the wolf-headed wood thrush is a unique species, or simply a variant of the parent stock. There is an excellent chance of spotting one of the more spectacular, if we may use that word, mutants, such as glow-in-the-dark grosbeaks, two-headed tundra swans, and metalpeckers. Your Geiger counter will be invaluable in alerting you to the presence of such.

Listen carefully for cues that alert you to the presence of shyer creatures such as the Bard Owl, which can be heard in woodlands muttering quotations from Shakespeare, or Moot Swans, often heard debating among themselves in secluded lakes or ponds.

If you are travelling through swampy areas, you might be fortunate enough to find a Blue Heron. These birds are likely to be more despondent than usual due to the precipitous decline in the frog population.

I mentioned birding gear, but I would be remiss in not commenting upon suggested safety measures. During your forays, do be alert for droppings from the mutated species particularly, as they tend to have a less than salutary effect on vehicle paint, asphalt, or human skin. For this reason, you may wish to invest in all-terrain body armor and Level 9 Protection footwear and gloves before you venture out. Respirators, of course, are essential, as is a healthy supply of industrial-strength insect repellent to deter the dragonfly-sized mosquitoes lurking in the underbrush. While it's true that purple martins, having increased in size in accordance with the mosquitoes, continue to make inroads on the insect population, they have a lot of eating yet to do.

But don't dismay. What could be more pleasant than spending some outdoor time, even if you're covered so thoroughly you can't feel the breeze, and there's no fresh air to speak of?

So, here's to an excellent count day! Do know that your efforts are appreciated.

Did I hear someone ask whether I'd be participating in this year's event? Erm—unfortunately, I'm afraid I'll be tied to my desk summarizing data. Pity, that. But do enjoy yourselves. Wish I could join you. . .

About the Author

Lisa Timpf is a former HR and communications professional who lives in Simcoe, Ontario. An avid bird-watcher, she has participated in the Great Backyard Bird Count, the Baillie Birdathon, and the Feederwatch program, although she has never spotted the rarer species mentioned in this piece. Her writing has appeared in *New Myths, The Martian Wave, Outposts of Beyond,* and the *Mother's Revenge* and *Dogs of War* anthologies.

*****~~~~*****

Credits and Acknowledgments

Cover image and design – Keely Rew
Podcast production – Andrew Cairns
Readers – Andrew Cairns, Genevieve L. Mattern, Tom Parker, Inken Purvis, Keely Rew, Leonard Sitongia
Editor and Publisher – Juliana Rew

*****~~~~~*****

Discover other titles by Third Flatiron:

(1) Over the Brink: Tales of Environmental Disaster
(2) A High Shrill Thump: War Stories
(3) Origins: Colliding Causalities
(4) Universe Horribilis
(5) Playing with Fire
(6) Lost Worlds, Retraced
(7) Redshifted: Martian Stories
(8) Astronomical Odds
(9) Master Minds
(10) Abbreviated Epics
(11) The Time It Happened
(12) Only Disconnect
(13) Ain't Superstitious
(14) Third Flatiron's Best of 2015
(15) It's Come to Our Attention
(16) Hyperpowers
(17) Keystone Chronicles
(18) Principia Ponderosa
(19) Cat's Breakfast
(20) Strange Beasties
(21) Third Flatiron Best of 2017
(22) Monstrosities

THIRD FLATIRON
www.thirdflatiron.com

www.ingramcontent.com/pod-product-compliance
Lightning Source LLC
Chambersburg PA
CBHW071243130626
46556CB00003B/1148